"You held my ha̶   him, "just as you are aung now, all but pulling me along in your hurry to escape Miss B."

"And what was the result of that escape? Did we find a secluded corner and a few moments of privacy?"

Ben watched the color creep into her face, and he knew the instant she recalled the kiss. "You need not answer," he said, "for your face gives you away." He lifted his hand and touched her temple, smoothing his fingertips slowly down to her jaw, enjoying the satiny feel of her skin. "Did I steal a kiss?" he whispered.

Phoebe did not think she had ever experienced anything as wonderful as the feel of Ben's fingertips sliding across her skin. When he asked her about the kiss, she held her breath, unmoving, all but willing him to steal another. In the silence that followed, he searched her eyes, as if judging her receptivity. Then he leaned toward her until he was so close she could feel the warmth of his breath against her lips.

"Shall I steal another?" he whispered.

The Rake's Fiancée

Martha Kirkland

A SIGNET BOOK

SIGNET
Published by New American Library, a division of
Penguin Putnam Inc., 375 Hudson Street,
New York, New York 10014, U.S.A.
Penguin Books Ltd, 27 Wrights Lane,
London W8 5TZ, England
Penguin Books Australia Ltd, Ringwood,
Victoria, Australia
Penguin Books Canada Ltd, 10 Alcorn Avenue,
Toronto, Ontario, Canada M4V 3B2
Penguin Books (N.Z.) Ltd, 182–190 Wairau Road,
Auckland 10, New Zealand

Penguin Books Ltd, Registered Offices:
Harmondsworth, Middlesex, England

First published by Signet, an imprint of New American Library,
a division of Penguin Putnam Inc.

First Printing, June 2001
10 9 8 7 6 5 4 3 2 1

To three of my cousins:
Mary Ann Townsend,
Margaret McCord Newett,
and Kathy Milton Griffith

Prologue

London, May, 1806 . . .

While Lieutenant George Alfred Bennett Holden made his offer of marriage, Miss Phoebe Catherine Lowell, the young lady who had come to fill his thoughts to the exclusion of all others, stood beside the long, narrow window that looked out onto Upper Brook Street in Grosvenor Square. She had not said a word since the lieutenant entered the rented town house and began his declaration. Instead, she gazed out onto the rain-soaked cobbled street, her back straight and unnaturally rigid, while her long, slender fingers twisted the gold tassel that held back the slightly worn green velvet drapery.

Though perplexed by the lady's rigid posture and her stony silence, the young gentleman persevered, for his beloved was obviously nervous, as was he. "To put it simply, Phoebe, my sweet, I adore you. I have loved you almost from the first moment I saw you, and if you will consent to be my bride, you will make me the happiest man on earth."

At last, his beloved abandoned the tassel and turned to face the lieutenant. If she was nervous, she hid it well, for when she spoke, her manner was cool, her voice calm. "Though I am sensible, sir, of the honor you do me by making me this offer, I fear I cannot accept."

"What!"

Unable to credit the reliability of his ears, Ben stared at the beautiful face of the lady he loved. Was she in jest? She must be. She had to be! And yet, the soft, youthful contours of her cheeks did not display the beguiling dimples that were the envy of every other young lady that Season, nor did her gray eyes show even a spark of the teasing light that was so much a part of her.

For Ben, asking Phoebe if she would accept his hand in marriage had been a mere formality. After all, he and Phoebe had an understanding. He loved her and she loved him; she had as much as told him so not fourteen hours ago at Lady Fitzpatrick's musicale. "My love," he said, "this is not amusing. I am in earnest. Do not make sport of me."

Phoebe's countenance remained cool, her words formal. "I, too, am in earnest. You made me an offer, Lieutenant, and I have refused it."

"But, why?"

"I am persuaded we would not suit. Can we not leave it at that?"

Hell, no, we cannot leave it at that!

Ben only just controlled his temper. Who was this stranger spouting platitudes at him? Certainly not the fun-loving nineteen-year-old who had been his friend, his confidante, his almost constant companion for the past two months of the Season. Ben wanted to shake her. To kiss her senseless. Anything to get her to show some reaction other than this damned cool detachment. "Phoebe, this is me. Ben. The man who loves you. The man you have given every reason to believe means as much to you as you mean to him."

"If I have misled you in any way, Lieutenant Holden, please accept my apologies. I pray you do not force me to say more."

"If you have misled me? Phoebe, what is this all

about? And why are you talking in that stilted manner, calling me Lieutenant Holden? You speak as though we are strangers. As though you do not know me."

"Which, it seems, sir, I do not."

"Damnation, Phoebe, what the devil are you—"

"How dare you curse at me!"

At last her eyes showed a bit of animation.

Encouraged, Ben begged her pardon. "Forgive me, my love, but I—"

"And do not call me your love! You would be wise to save such honeyed phrases for Miss Wadington and her thirty thousand pounds."

"Miss Wadington? Is that what this snub is all about?" Ben breathed a sigh of relief. Jealousy was an emotion he could readily understand. Not that his lovely Phoebe had anything to be jealous of—not now, not ever. Suppressing a smile at her naïveté, he said, "Sweet, adorable goose! Surely you do not think for one moment that I care for Miss—"

"What happened?" Phoebe asked, her tone so icy cold it chilled the air. "Do not tell me the heiress has already turned you down? If that is the case, then I say, 'Good for her.' Like me, Miss Wadington must have heard about all the others."

Phoebe's voice broke on the final word, and tears flooded her eyes. It was the first promising sign Ben had seen since he walked into the drawing room, and he moved toward her, his arms outstretched, ready to kiss away all her doubts. "Sweetheart, if some busybody has been filling your ears with lies, please allow me to set your mind at—"

"Do not!" she said holding her hand up, palm toward him, to halt him before he reached her. "I had the truth from my uncle, and he would not lie to me."

"Sir Lawrence? But I spoke to your uncle just last evening, and he gave me leave to call upon you today, to ask for your hand. After approving my suit, surely he would not then speak ill of me."

Though Phoebe's eyes were still damp with tears, her posture was once again rigid. "Is speaking the truth the same as speaking ill? I think not. As my guardian, Uncle Lawrence told me only what he felt I needed to know. You are a rake, Ben Holden, a known seducer of women, and if you were the last man on earth, I would not consent to marry you."

It was Ben's turn to stiffen. "And this is your final word? Take care, madam, for if you turn me away, it is for good."

At his ultimatum, something showed in her eyes—a hint of vulnerability, perhaps?—and Phoebe reached her hand out as if to touch him. Apparently thinking better of it, she stepped back before her fingers made contact with the sleeve of his coat.

Phoebe stared at Ben's sleeve; then, unable to stop herself, she allowed her gaze to slip down to his wrist and his hand. His fingers were long and supple, yet there was a strength to his hands, a strength that had always teased at her imagination, more than once figuring in her girlish fantasies. Recalling one fantasy in particular, her entire body grew heated.

She lifted her gaze to Ben's handsome face, searching the depths of his dark brown eyes—eyes whose smoldering glances could send chills of delight down her spine. Silently, she begged him to deny the accusation that he was a womanizer. "Perhaps there is some mitigating circumstance my uncle failed to mention. If . . . if that is the case, and you have an explanation—"

"Madam," Ben replied, his voice ominously quiet, "I never explain. One either takes me on faith, or one does not."

Phoebe wanted to take him on faith. Her heart fairly ached to believe he was everything she had thought him to be. And yet, her uncle would not lie. If he said Ben was a rake, then it must be so.

For an indefinite length of time emotion-charged silence hung between them. Phoebe waited for Ben to say something—anything—to reassure her that she could trust in his love. Apparently, he waited as well for some show of faith from her. When none was forthcoming, his eyes turned glacial, chilling her to the bone.

"Very well," he said, making her a formal bow, "pray forgive me for having taken up your time, Miss Lowell. You may rest assured, it will not happen again." With that, he turned and walked away, the only indication of his anger the window-rattling strength with which he slammed the drawing room door.

Chapter One

Coalport, Shropshire, February, 1814 . . .

Phoebe Lowell rinsed the pale pink paint from her brush and set it upside down in the jar at the edge of her small worktable. The half-finished plate she laid carefully on the cloth-covered refectory table behind her, being mindful not to let it touch any of the other plates already placed there during the morning. She had spent the last five hours painting roses, and she was heartily sick of the pink swirls, the green leaves, and the brown thorns on the lighter brown stems. Monday she would apply the gilding to the fluted edges of the porcelain, and when that step was completed, all twelve plates would be fired a second time, thereby making the gold fuse with the colors of the roses and the cobalt background to become permanent.

For today, however, her work was done. Saturday was a half day, and the bell had already sounded indicating the closing of the Coalport Pottery Works until Monday morning at seven.

Today was her birthday, and Phoebe had plans for the remainder of the afternoon. A woman did not turn twenty-seven every day, and she meant to celebrate, if only with a solitary walk to Wenlock Gorge, where she could eat her midday meal in privacy and blessed silence.

Privacy was a rare commodity at Mrs. Curdy's, where Phoebe shared one of the six small bedchambers with three other females. Since all the females who resided at the Widow Curdy's were porcelain painters, Phoebe saw them at the factory as well as during her evening hours. After hearing the same gossip, the same complaints, the same conversation day in and day out, it was no wonder that she lived for the peaceful hours of her Saturday afternoon walks.

Six months earlier, when Phoebe had returned to the employment agency on Fulham Road in London, after being turned out from her third position as companion to an elderly lady, she had all but leapt at the opportunity to travel north into Shropshire. Understandably, Mr. Bishop, the middle-aged director of the agency, had voiced his doubts about a young lady of Phoebe's upbringing being able to withstand the rigors of a job in a factory, but Phoebe had insisted that she wanted to try.

"I am stronger than I look, I assure you. And since I have neither the education necessary to make me a successful governess, nor the submissive disposition required of a companion, I have given up all thought of applying for any more similar positions. I am, however, a better than average painter."

"But my dear Miss Lowell, a bit of watercoloring to pass a lazy afternoon is not at all the same thing as sitting for sixty hours a week in a factory, painting the same picture day after day, year after year, until your eyesight or your fingers finally give out on you."

The balding gentleman removed the pince-nez spectacles from the bridge of his long, pointed nose. "And, of course, there is the matter of the social disparity between yourself and those workers with whom you will be obliged to work and live."

Phoebe had felt her face grow warm. "As to that,

sir, there is no social disparity. The people I will meet are obliged to earn their daily bread, just as I am obliged to earn mine."

"But if Sir Lawrence were here, I am certain he would say that employment in such a place was beneath the dignity of the Lowell family."

At the mention of her uncle, Phoebe had stretched to her full five feet, five inches, her shoulders back, and her teeth clamped shut to keep her from giving vent to some of the feelings pent up inside her. "I *have* no more family," she said. "My parents left me when I was but twelve years old, and—"

"Left you? Forgive me, but I understood that Sir George and Lady Lowell were killed in a boating accident."

Phoebe felt heat surge to her face. "Yes, of course they were. That is what I meant to say."

When Mr. Bishop made no reply, Phoebe continued. "As for my uncle's notion of family dignity, I wish you will tell me, sir, where is the dignity in putting a bullet in one's brain? Had Uncle Lawrence possessed the courage to face life and find a way to repay his ever-mounting gaming debts, he would still be alive, and I would not now be alone in the world and in the position of hiring myself out for fifteen pounds per annum."

That argument being unanswerable, Mr. Bishop had finally given in and bought Phoebe a stagecoach ticket to Shrewsbury. As well, he had advanced her the few shillings needed to defray the cost of the rented gig that conveyed her and her trunk the remaining fourteen miles north. Phoebe had not been the first young woman to answer the advertisement for porcelain painters, so the driver of the gig had known exactly where to take her. The gig rattled across the famous iron bridge to Coalport, then it con-

tinued through the narrow, winding streets to Mrs.
Alberta Curdy's plain, red-brick house.

The dormitory—never mind the fact that the
Quaker lady called it by the more genteel name of residence hall—was as neat as a pin, but sparsely decorated, with not one picture nor a single statue in the
entire house. Not so much as a piece of the beautifully
decorated Coalport pottery made its way through the
doors of the residence, though the factory was but
two blocks away.

"Idolatry," the bone-thin, gray-clad lady replied in
answer to all inquiries regarding painted plates and
decorated statues, and that one word sufficed to end
all conversation on the subject.

Now, six months later, Phoebe had more or less settled in to her job at the pottery works; in fact, she actually liked being employed. There was something
rather invigorating about having work to do, and it
was rewarding to see a lovely dish or vase come out
of the kiln and know its beauty was, in no small part,
a result of her skill. And, of course, nothing could
match the excitement of receiving her monthly pay,
meager though it might be.

Naturally, this was not the life Phoebe Lowell had
pictured for herself eight years ago, when she had her
one and only Season in Town. At that time, she had
hoped, even expected, to fall in love and marry. All
she had ever wanted was a home and family of her
own. And yet, working at the factory was not so bad.

Mr. Abraham Darby, the builder of the iron bridge,
and the founder of the pottery works, had seen to it
that his factory was as modern and as up to date as
his money and British ingenuity could make it. Windows were plentiful, and the entire place was lit by
burning hydrogen gas, which made the workrooms
light as day. Furthermore, the gentleman was a
Quaker, like Mrs. Curdy, and he insisted that his em-

ployees have Saturday afternoons off so they could see to all necessary personal chores prior to the Sabbath, thus leaving their Sundays free for meditation and the seeking of the "Inner Light."

Reared Church of England, Phoebe attended Sunday services at Saint Anne's, an observance she would not have ignored no matter where she worked, but she refused to waste her Saturday afternoons in mundane chores. When she had arrived in Shropshire last September, the trees had been in magnificent color, and on her first half-day she had made short work of the three miles that took her back across the iron bridge to what soon became her own private haven, Wenlock Gorge. And now, with thoughts of the quiet gorge in mind, Phoebe hurried her steps along the winding streets to Mrs. Curdy's.

The widow set strict rules for herself and for those who lived under her roof, and one of those rules was punctuality for meals. She served the midday meal at exactly half past twelve, and anyone who was not seated at one of the two long oak tables in time for the asking of the Lord's Grace, was obliged to take her meal in the kitchen, or else sit in the parlor until the others had finished and their hostess had said the closing prayer.

On this particular day, Pheobe chose to go to the kitchen, where she wrapped a piece of hard cheese and two slices of freshly baked bread in a napkin. "When I saw you were not at table on time," said the young maid of all work, "I set aside a piece of hot gingerbread for you. You want I should wrap it up as well, miss?"

Phoebe smiled at the girl, whose strong accent on words containing the letter "R" gave evidence of her Shropshire upbringing. "Abby, you are a dear to look out for me."

The red-haired maid blushed as only those of her

hair coloring could do. Pushing the mobcap back off her forehead, she went to the larder and brought back a saucer containing a large square of fragrant gingerbread and set it on the scrubbed deal table.

"Thank you," Phoebe said.

"You're welcome, I'm sure, miss, though it's not near what I would like to do for you, you being such a lady and all. And don't be saying you're no different from them others here at Mrs. Curdy's, for I've eyes in me head, and I can see you're quality make."

"No, really, Abby, I—"

"Protest all you want, miss, but I been working for Mrs. Curdy since I was eleven, and you're the first of her guests ever remembered me on Boxing Day. I wear the lovely lace fichu you embroidered for me every Sunday, and you should see me friend, Lucy. She's so jealous she's pea green, on account of her never having anything half so delicate herself."

Having uncorked her long-bottled appreciation, the maid appeared disinclined to reapply the stopper. "Nor have I forgot the two shillings you give the apothecary last month for the cough syrup for me mam and the three little ones at home."

It was Phoebe's turn to blush. "I was happy to hear that your family recovered so quickly." Hoping to turn the conversation, she asked the girl what all the bustle was about in the dining room. "For I detect an inordinate amount of whispering and giggling going on at the tables."

"As well you might, miss, for everyone's agog with the news."

"Oh?" Phoebe said, slipping the two wrapped food packets into the deep pockets of the paint-spattered white coverall she wore at the pottery works. "What news is that?"

"It's his lordship. Or the new lordship, I should say. They received word at Holden House that he's on his way to Shropshire at last. It's been over a year since the old baron went to his maker, and the new baron is finally coming to see what needs to be done to make the place fit to live in. Not but what he'll have his work cut out for him, I'm thinking. According to Mrs. Curdy's sister-in-law, her as is housekeeper at the House, the old gentleman was a bit peculiar, and he let the place go to wrack and ruin, not a groat spent on it this quarter century and more."

Phoebe heard little of what was said. From the moment the maid had mentioned the heir to Holden House, all else had left Phoebe's head. Naturally, it had come as a shock to her, shortly after her own arrival in Shropshire, to discover the identity of the sixth Baron Holden, and she had hoped his long delay in taking possession of his newly inherited estate might continue indefinitely.

Of course, in this view she was alone. The new Lord Holden's actions—or lack thereof—were the principal topic of conversation at any gathering, and everyone in Coalport was eager to see him take up residence.

The old baron had been a recluse—some said even a bit dotty—and he had discouraged visits from what little family he possessed. As a result, when the eighty-five-year-old bachelor had finally put his spoon in the wall, not even his servants knew anything of the new heir save his name.

"George Alfred Bennett Holden," Abby said, as if reading Phoebe's thoughts. "Decorated in the war, he was, and retired a major from the Royal Regiment of Artillery."

Pheobe had heard all this before, but it did not stop the maid from continuing her recitation of every last detail known of the new baron. "According to Mrs. Curdy, his lordship served under Sir Arthur Wellesley in the Peninsular War. That was from ought-seven to thirteen, until he received a wound of some kind and was sent home to England where he could be nursed back to health."

The young servant sighed. Then a moment later an idea appeared to take hold of her and she shuddered. "Oh, miss, I just had the most awful thought. What if his lordship's wound left him—you know—so's his face frightens little children, sending them screaming in the streets?"

Phoebe sincerely hoped that was not the case; for his lordship's sake as well as for the composure of the local children. For a few seconds, she allowed herself to recall the handsome face of the twenty-three-year-old lieutenant who had stolen her heart at the first party of her come-out. He had been tall and slender, with dark brown hair, and even darker brown eyes— eyes that had seemed to look into her very soul—and he had possessed the chiseled features of a Greek statue.

His good looks, coupled with an abundance of charm and a heart-stopping smile, had made him the object of attention from half the young ladies brought to Town for the Season, Phoebe included.

She had fallen in love with him within minutes of meeting him, and Ben had fallen for her with equal speed. Or so he had said. Two months later, however, her uncle had informed her that Ben Holden was a rake, and that his reputation with women was legend. When Phoebe had confronted Ben with the accusation, he had not denied it.

Of course, at that time the lieutenant had nothing to recommend him but his charm and his pretty uniform. Ben Holden lived on his officer's pay, augmented by an admittedly small inheritance from his maternal grandfather. He had never misrepresented himself on that score. Oddly enough, not once during their acquaintance had there been any mention of an elderly uncle in Shropshire—dotty or otherwise—and Phoebe still wondered why Ben had not mentioned a peer with a prosperous estate that might one day be his.

Such information might have influenced her uncle's opinion of Ben as a suitor.

Naturally, Sir Lawrence had wished Phoebe to marry advantageously, but there was nothing so unusual about that. Was there? As her guardian, it was his duty to look out for her welfare. Over the years, however, Phoebe had often wondered if her uncle's financial difficulties had anything to do with prompting him to reveal Ben's reputation with the ladies.

It was a bit late to wonder about that now, of course.

As often happened when she thought of Ben Holden, an odd pang of loss assailed Phoebe—loss of the fun-loving, handsome young man who had once captured her heart. Had that person ever really existed? Had he been a rake all along, merely amusing himself at her expense, or had her uncle lied for his own purposes? In truth, after all this time it no longer mattered, and like the young maid, Phoebe sighed. Regardless of her uncle's motives, Ben was out of her life. He had been for almost eight years.

Phoebe was now a painter in a pottery works, a factory worker. But even if she were not thus employed, and still moved in the circle of society to which Ben, as a wealthy baron, would be most welcome, it would not signify. She had burned her bridges that morning in London when she had called him a rake and refused his proposal. One had only to recall the cold anger in his eyes when he took his leave of her to know that if there was one man in the entire country who had no wish ever to see her again, that man was Ben Holden.

"But he's not likely to be traveling today," Abby

said, bringing Phoebe's reminiscences to an abrupt halt, "not with it being so cold out."

Happy to impart a further bit of information, she added, "As far as anyone in these parts can recall, this is the coldest winter in twenty-five years. And not just here. Why, would you believe it, miss, according to Reverend Gladney, whose brother saw it with his own eyes, the Thames froze over solid last week, and what must them Londoners do but hold a fair for five days right out on the ice!"

The servant sighed again. "Now there's a sight I'd give me Sunday hat to see. Jugglers and strolling minstrels, and people by the thousands, all walking under London Bridge."

Phoebe, who had crossed London Bridge many times, and was familiar with the depth and breadth of the river, shivered just thinking of so much ice. "Brrr."

"Wouldn't it be something like, miss, if the Severn froze under Iron Bridge? Happen we could hold a fair here in Coalport."

Far from charmed by the prospect, Phoebe said, "Has it ever frozen before?"

Abby shrugged. "Don't know about the river, miss, but the bridge ices over at least once every winter. Sometimes it's so bad a body can't walk across it without risking life and limb."

The two were quiet for a moment, then Abby said, "If I'm any judge, it's coming on to snow again. By nightfall, happen we'll be up to our ankles in fresh powder. And if you'll forgive me poking my nose in, miss, on account of I know you like to walk all the way to the gorge, you'd be wise not to chance venturing so far today."

Though the birthday girl thanked her for the warning, Phoebe had no intention of forgoing her afternoon of privacy. "I promise to be vigilant," she said, "and I will start back at sight of the first snowflake."

Having made her promise, Phoebe gave a quick wave in Abby's direction, then hurried up to her room to change from her work clothes into a warm, merino wool dress and leather walking boots.

A quarter of an hour later, bundled up against the cold, with a knitted scarf around her neck and the hood of her heavy, dark blue wool cloak tied snugly beneath her chin, Phoebe slipped out the rear door at Mrs. Curdy's. Though eager to be at the gorge, she slowed to a respectful pace as she passed the neat Quaker cemetery where her landlady's husband was laid to rest.

Moments later, Phoebe took a short cut beneath a covered passage between two red-brick shops, and once she emerged from the shut, she hurried past row upon row of red-brick houses interspersed with a few of those low, crooked, half-timbered black-and-white houses that had been built during Tudor times. Feeling freer by the minute, she continued down the winding street that led to the Iron Bridge. The bridge had been constructed one mile downstream from Coalport, and as always, before crossing to the other side of the Severn, Phoebe paused a moment to gaze at this modern marvel.

Built by Mr. Abraham Darby some thirty-five years earlier, the impressive arched bridge, which was the first of its kind in the world, gave access to Coalport to the east. To the west of the bridge were steep-sided banks clothed in dark green woodland, and it was to those woods and beyond that Phoebe was headed, her ultimate goal Wenlock Gorge.

Some twenty minutes after crossing the bridge, Phoebe followed a rutted country lane that led gradually uphill. This being a sparsely populated area, she passed no cottages, just a thick copse of evergreen trees blended with a few larch, with their clean, straight trunks, and several Norway maples with their smooth, pale gray bark.

Once past the copse, she paused to catch her breath, leaning against a low brick wall that snaked its way for perhaps a quarter mile along the lane. Holden House, the only home for miles around, lay beyond that wall, at the end of a crushed-stone carriageway that curved its way behind a stand of trees.

From the lane, Phoebe could see no more of the house, which was L-shaped, than a bit of the steep-pitched roofline, and she was reasonably certain that no one inside the house could see her sitting on the wall. Still, now that the new baron was to take up residence, Phoebe would be obliged to find another haven for her solitary walks. She would have to abandon Wenlock Gorge, for she could not have Ben Holden discover her walking by his estate. Chances were she would meet him sooner or later in the village, but she did not want him to think she was trying to renew their acquaintance by putting herself in his path.

Nothing could be further from the truth.

No matter what her uncle's motives had been for telling her of Ben's reputation for wooing women, then tiring of them and seeking new conquests, Ben never denied the accusation. He knew she was an orphan, and he must have known how much Phoebe needed to hear him say it was all a fabrication—how much she needed reassurance from him that he would never leave her. And yet he had said nothing. Convicted by his own silence, Ben Holden had left the house on Grosvenor Square, slamming the door behind him.

If he was a rake eight years ago, more than likely he was a rake still, for such men did not change for the better. Nor had Phoebe changed. At least, her convictions had not. She had wanted no part of a rake when she was a girl, and she wanted nothing to do with such a man now.

Not if her life depended upon it!

Chapter Two

As always, Wenlock Gorge was more dramatic than beautiful, with its steep, heather-covered escarpment that stretched for perhaps fifteen miles; and yet, it never failed to enchant Phoebe. Not that she dared go all the way to the edge. She found it quite dramatic enough sitting a dozen feet back. And even though the wind blew icy cold, burning her cheeks and bringing tears to her eyes, she huddled inside her warm cloak, delighting in the solitude—a solitude disturbed only by the occasional sight of a bird.

While she ate her simple birthday meal, Phoebe watched a colorful kestrel soaring high above the gorge, surveying the tree-lined valley below in search of his own dinner. At times he seemed almost not to move. A wonder to behold, he was suspended in air, supported by his outspread tail, and by an almost imperceptible quivering of his red and brown wings.

He must have spotted likely prey, for in an instant he veered right, then swooped downward, beauty in motion, and once he was out of sight, Phoebe sighed. "Thank you," she said, "for my lovely birthday performance."

Wanting to prolong her solitude, and unwilling to return to the village one minute before it was absolutely necessary, Phoebe drew her cloak ever closer around her, and with her feet tucked beneath the warmth of her wool skirt, she leaned her back against the trunk of a stunted larch and watched for the reappearance of the kestrel. The bird, unaware of its admiring audience, did not return, and soon Phoebe felt her eyelids grow heavy.

After six months at Mrs. Curdy's, Phoebe still had not learned to sleep soundly with two other people in the bedchamber, so she was always just a bit sleepy. Today was no different, and in time she gave in to temptation and allowed her eyelids to close.

Just for a minute or two.

Phoebe had napped on numerous other visits here at the gorge, but today, when she awoke, she realized just how dangerous a nap could be. First and foremost, she was too near the edge of the gorge to allow for such foolish behavior. Second, this was not October, with its autumn crispness, but the middle of February, and the temperature had dropped rapidly while Phoebe slept.

Just as Abby had predicted, the snow had returned, and it was coming down fast and thick. So thick, in fact, that Phoebe could no longer see to the rim of the gorge. Worse yet, it must have been snowing for an hour or more, for the ground was completely covered, and Phoebe was all but buried in white.

Buried!

The very word struck fear in her, and she attempted to spring to her feet. Unfortunately, her legs had been tucked beneath her for too long, and they, too, had gone to sleep. When she attempted to stand, her legs refused to hold her, and with a gasp, she pitched face first into the soft, powdery snow. She was unharmed, but the sensation of falling when she knew herself to be only a few feet from the edge of the gorge left her shaking with fright.

Warning herself to remain calm, Phoebe brushed the snow from her face and hands and tried once again to stand. This time, she became thoroughly entangled in the yards of material in her skirt and cloak, and the more she struggled, the more tangled she became.

At last she made it to her feet, but not without mishap. Pins and needles jabbed her feet and legs, leaving her wobbly as a new colt, and when she tried to make her way around to the other side of the larch, she stumbled over a hidden root and banged her left knee against the tree trunk.

"It wanted only that!" she muttered, rubbing the injured area and cursing herself for having been so foolish as to get caught in a winter storm.

As she stared at the deluge of white before her, a lump rose in her throat. Things were going from bad to worse. The thickly falling snow had already obscured the path that led back to the lane; Phoebe could barely see four feet in front of her; and now her knee ached so badly she was unable to walk without limping.

Her lips began to tremble. Though she continued forward toward what she hoped was the path, she moved much too slowly, and she knew if she did not pick up her pace, she would never be able to walk the three miles and more to the village before nightfall.

Regrettably, within less than five minutes it became all too obvious that if she had all day, she could not walk three miles. The way her knee ached, Phoebe would be lucky if she managed half a mile. And yet, she must manage it. She was in a deserted area, with no place to turn for help, and once the light failed, she would be unable to see her hand in front of her face.

The lump in her throat doubled in size, threatening to choke her. She had no idea how to survive out-of-doors in a winter storm, and if she got lost and was forced to spend the night in the woods, she would freeze to death before morning!

Fear being a strong motivator, Phoebe kept walking, albeit slowly, and at last she reached the lane. At least, she hoped it was the lane. Her senses told her it was so, and she had no recourse but to follow her instincts and continue putting one foot in front of the other.

She had no idea how far she had traveled when she stumbled again, only this time the thing she fell against was no tree. The object was no more than two feet tall, and unless Pheobe was mistaken, it was made of brick. More excited than she would have thought possible, she began to brush away the snow, and within seconds she found what she had been almost too frightened to hope for—a brick wall. But not just any brick wall. Phoebe had sat on this particular wall often enough to know that just beyond it was the crushed-stone carriageway that led to Holden House.

Ben Holden's home was the last place on earth she wanted to be, even if he was not in residence, but at the moment she had no other choice. She was already so numbed by the cold that she could no longer feel her toes, and if she did not get indoors soon, she would surely fall victim to frostbite.

Thoughts of a frozen nose or, Heaven forbid! the loss of one or more fingers, proved sufficient incentive to hurry her up the carriageway to the thick, double doors of the large L-shaped house. Shivering with a combination of cold and mortification at having to beg shelter at Holden House, Phoebe lifted the heavy iron knocker and let it fall against the iron plate. A dull sound reverberated in the hushed silence.

When a full two minutes passed, and no one came to the door, Phoebe panicked. What if no one was home? Fear erased every vestige of her mortification, and Phoebe sounded the knocker again and again, not stopping until she finally heard someone struggling with the heavy iron latch bolt.

"Damnation," a man said, "what's all the racket? Can't a man eat 'is tea in peace?"

It never occurred to Phoebe that whoever answered her knock would not let her in. Of course, there was no way she could have anticipated the hostility of the thick-set individual who finally worked the bolt free and opened one of the doors a few inches, just wide enough to stare at her through bloodshot eyes. Surely this was not the butler, for he wore a food-stained smock instead of a uniform, he reeked of onions and ale, and if his hard, unsmiling face had seen a razor that week, Phoebe would be surprised.

He looked Phoebe up and down, and if a person can be said to snarl, he did. "What do you want?"

"I want in," she replied. "I am desperately cold, and I—"

"Lord 'Olden b'aint 'ere," he said. "If you've business with 'im, come back next week."

Phoebe could not believe her ears. Surely the man did not expect her to go away—not in such a storm as this? Apparently that was exactly what he expected, for to Phoebe's horror, he began to close the door.

Terrified, she threw the full force of her weight against the heavy wood and pushed. "Stop!" she shouted. "You must let me in."

The servant pushed back, almost dislodging her. "I told you, 'is lordship b'aint 'ere."

"I know that," Phoebe said, desperately searching for some story that would gain her admittance. "Lord Holden sent me."

The man blinked, as if to clear his ale-fogged head, and though he eased his hold on the door, he still barred the way. "What do you mean, 'e sent you? Why would 'is lordship do that?"

Recalling what Abby had said about the previous baron allowing the house to go to wrack and ruin, Phoebe said, "His lordship wants me to look over the

house. To . . . er . . . to make an inventory of the furnishings."

The servant's eyes widened in alarm, and for some
reason, Phoebe was reminded of a fox caught outside
the poultry house, turkey feathers still stuck to its
muzzle. After a moment, however, the look was gone,
replaced by one of suspicion. "'Is lordship's letter
didn't say nothing about an inventory."

"All the same, he—"

"Curious," the man continued, "'im sending a female to do the job."

It was a valid point, and anyone other than this
slovenly excuse for a servant would have known im-
mediately that no gentleman would send a lone female to inventory his furnishings. "Curious or not,"
she said, braving it out, "Lord Holden sent me." *But
why?* Hoping to forestall the next question, Phoebe
racked her brain for a plausible excuse for her presence. "Because," she added, "I will be living here."

The man's mouth fell open. "Living 'ere?"

"Yes," she continued in a rush. "I . . . I am Lord
Holden's fiancée!"

That final word proved as much a surprise to
Phoebe as it did to the butler. Fortunately, it had the
desired effect, for the man opened the door and
stepped aside. Not willing to give him a chance to
change his mind, Phoebe hurried past him, more
grateful than she could say to be in out of the cold.

Not that the large, round vestibule, with its green-
veined marble floor was all that warm. It had a decidedly unlived-in feeling, and Phoebe had no desire to
linger. Actually, she hoped to be shown abovestairs
before the man asked after her luggage. "I am quite
fatigued," she said, feigning a yawn, "so if you will
show me to one of the guest bedchambers, I will retire
for the evening."

"Guest bedchamber?"

It was a simple request, and one that should not have occasioned any particular surprise, but once again the servant had that look of the fox caught raiding the poultry house.

"It need not be one of the principal rooms," she said. "Anything will do."

"B'aint but one bedchamber available. T'others been closed off for years."

"As I said, any room will do."

When the man hesitated, indecision in his bloodshot eyes, Phoebe borrowed a page from the book of her last employer, an overbearing old lady who thought servants were a lower order of humanity. Looking down her nose at the man, Phoebe used her frostiest tone. "Now, sirrah!"

Reacting to the authority in her tone, the fellow attempted a bow, nearly toppling over with the effort. "Yes, miss. This way, if you please." Without another word, he turned and walked none too steadily toward the rear of the vestibule, his wobbly gait verifying Phoebe's suspicion that he was inebriated.

After the whiteness of the outside world, the vestibule seemed uncommonly dim, so Phoebe saw very little of the two ground-floor rooms they passed. She did notice, however, that one of the rooms appeared sparsely furnished, surprisingly so. She saw only one or two pieces of furniture, and those were beneath Holland covers. As well, there was none of the usual bric-a-brac in sight, and along one wall, dust-bordered squares showed clearly where paintings had once hung.

Empty niches were in evidence in the walls of the vestibule and along the wide, cantilevered staircase that led to the upper floors, causing Phoebe to reflect on the irony of the situation. If she had truly come to Holden House to take an inventory of the furnishings, it would have been a short one.

Why was the house so bare? Her fib notwithstanding, what went on in this house was no concern of hers, so Phoebe wisely kept her curiosity to herself. She wanted only a warm place to stay until morning, when she could see to return to the village.

The servant took forever to climb the first flight of the timeworn marble steps, and fearful that he might topple over in a drunken stupor and fall to his death, Phoebe told him he need not take her the rest of the way. "Merely tell me which door."

"That way," he said, pointing down the corridor to the left. "Last door on the right. It's the master bedchamber," he added, "but it's been tidied up since the old baron kicked the bucket."

Please, Heaven! Let that be true!

Nearly eight years of penury had rid Phoebe of many of her earlier notions of what was required for basic comfort, but she drew the line at sleeping on sheets that had been on the bed for a year. Especially sheets on which someone had died.

While the servant turned and half stumbled back down the stairs, Phoebe hurried along the corridor, past four other doors, to the bedchamber he had pointed out.

Gratefully, she opened the door, then closed it behind her. There was no key in the lock, and though she would have rested easier had she been able to lock the door, she was relieved to discover that the room had, indeed, been "tidied up." Dust-free, and as neat as a pin, it had probably been cleaned within the past few days, obviously in preparation for the arrival of the new Lord Holden.

A worn, though still handsome turkey carpet covered most of the wooden floor, and in the center of the carpet, taking up at least half the room, was the most enormous tester bed Phoebe had ever seen. Easily capable of sleeping four to six people, all of them lying sideways, the bed boasted faded, wine velvet drapery and thick, elaborately carved ebony posts.

To Phoebe's right was a door leading to a small dressing room, while to her left a handsome rosewood desk and a Windsor chair stood against the wall between two mullioned windows. On the desk's leather top sat a pretty cobalt blue candelabra and an ormolu mantel clock that must have been wound recently, for it ticked softly in the silence of the room. Next to the clock someone had placed a silver tray containing two small glasses and a crystal decanter filled with an amber liquid.

The fireplace had been swept clean and was laid with logs ready to be lit, but Phoebe did not take time to light a fire. She had long since grown accustomed to sleeping in an unheated room; besides, the snow on her clothing was melting, and the icy wetness was making her shiver uncontrollably. Needing to warm up quickly, she went to the small dressing room, stripped off her clothes and shoes, then spread her damp dress and cloak over a barber's chair where they would dry out by morning. Finally, wearing only her thin lawn shift and her drawers, she ran to the oversize bed and crawled beneath the covers.

The sheets were glacial, and Phoebe was too cold herself to warm them up. Finally, after several minutes of listening to her teeth chatter loud enough to wake the household, she decided the only thing that might get her blood flowing was a taste of that amber liquid in the decanter. The decision made, she threw back the heavy covers, ran across the floor to the desk, quickly filled one of the small glasses almost to the top, then hurried back to the bed.

Sitting up, with the covers pulled up to her chin, Phoebe sipped at the spirituous liquid. She had drunk champagne before, and liked the flavor and the bubbles, but whatever this stuff was—brandy, she supposed—it tasted vile. Within seconds, however, after only a few sips, she began to feel the alcohol stealing through her veins and warming her arms and legs. Encouraged, she forced herself to take several more sips, until even her toes felt as though they had begun to thaw.

Finally, after placing the nearly empty glass on the bedside table, Phoebe slid down once again beneath the covers, pulling them up over her ears. This time, the sheets did not seem nearly as glacial as before.

One last look toward the windows convinced her that she had been wise not to attempt to make it to the village. The wind had picked up and was howling like a banshee, the snow was coming down even thicker than before, and the last traces of late-afternoon light were fading, with darkness probably no more than half an hour away. Before long, partly because of the spirits she had drunk and partly because of the frightening ordeal of the storm, Phoebe slipped into a deep and dreamless sleep.

Or nearly dreamless.

At some time during the night, she had one of those dreams, the kind she never told anyone about. A dream in which a tall, dark-haired man with a candle entered the bedchamber. Moving quietly, he set the candle and a pocket pistol on the bedside table, then he removed his clothing, letting each piece fall to the floor until he was completely naked. His shoulders were wide, and his back was broad, and even in her dreams, Phoebe had never seen anyone so perfectly formed.

As always happened in her dreams, the man did not speak. Soundlessly, he blew out the candle flame, pushed aside the heavy velvet drapery, then crawled into the big bed and pulled the covers up to his neck. At first he slept on his right side, with his back to Phoebe, but after a time he turned toward the middle of the bed and slipped his arm around her waist, pulling her against his hard, naked body.

These sort of dreams proceeded in much this same fashion every time, with only slight variations, so Phoebe kept her eyes tightly shut, unashamedly giving herself up to the pleasurable sensation of being held close in a man's arms. Even if the man was merely a figment of her imagination.

She remained quite still, savoring the delicious warmth that coursed through her veins, unwilling to break the magic spell. Unfortunately, the spell was irrevocably broken when a deep, sleepy voice murmured close to her ear, shocking her awake in an instant. "Umm, sweetings," he said, "you smell good enough to eat."

Chapter Three

Ben Holden had been asleep for an hour or more when he turned onto his left side and slid toward the middle of the oversize bed. Though the carriage accident had happened earlier in the evening, his head stilled ached as though pugilists were inside it trying to punch their way out, and he hoped a new place on the pillow might lessen the throbbing behind his eyes. Unfortunately, he found no solace from the pain, only icy cold sheets.

When he would have turned back to his right, to that place he had already warmed with his body, he felt an unexpected source of warmth coming from the far side of the bed. Still more asleep than awake, he did not question the origin of the warmth; he merely followed his instincts and slid closer. To his delight, if not his surprise, the bed warmer was human, and most decidedly female.

At first he thought it must be Blanche, but when he slipped his arm around the slender waist, he discovered the female had none of Blanche's voluptuousness. Still, whoever she was—probably one of the serving wenches from the taproom belowstairs—she was an inviting armful, and Ben had no objections to sharing his bed with her. So long as she expected nothing more from him. At the moment, with his head threatening to explode atop his shoulders, he was of no more use to a woman than a eunuch.

He pulled the woman against him, molding her soft form to his. She came willingly, allowing herself to be gathered close, and in gratitude for her amiability and the sweet, fresh scent of lemon verbena that clung to her smooth skin, Ben murmured something complimentary into her ear.

He was on his way to drifting back to sleep, when the female suddenly stiffened like a piece of newly milled lumber. Moments later, he felt tentative fingers pressing into his forearm as if testing its solidity. Then, before he could even guess at her intent, the woman let out a high-pitched scream that threatened to split his skull in two.

Ben was still reeling from the painful effects of that scream, when his persecutor began to struggle as though he were holding her against her will. "Let me go!" she yelled. Obviously demented, she did not give him time to comply with the order before she dug her fingernails into his arm. Not content with shredding his skin, she began kicking at his shins.

Under normal circumstances, Ben might have enjoyed a friendly tussle, but in his present condition, the last thing he needed was a fight with some crazed she-cat. With no other thought than to protect himself, he caught one of her wrists in his hand, then he used his arm to pin her other wrist against her chest. When she continued to twist and squirm, he threw his leg over both of hers and pressed her into the mattress to quell any further resistance.

Still she fought him.

"Damnation, woman! Desist. I am injured, and in no condition to go another ten rounds with you. I have no wish to restrain you, but neither do I mean to let you inflict further pain on me."

Having made his position clear, he waited until the deranged female grew still, then he relaxed his arm and swung it upward, throwing back the covers.

"There," he said, removing his leg from across hers, "you are free to go."

Not waiting for further confirmation, she scrambled out of the bed and ran to the adjacent dressing room, where she seemed to be feeling around for something. It was pitch dark in there, and whatever it was she sought, she obviously did not find it, for she continued to move about, bumping into something in her haste and crying out in pain.

Ben was awake enough now to realize that he was no longer at the Tawny Lion in Shrewsbury, and that whoever the female was, she was not one of the serving wenches from the inn taproom. At her cry of pain, Ben rolled over onto his right side and began to feel around on the bedside table for the phosphorus box he remembered seeing there before he had extinguished the candle and crawled into bed.

Could this day get any worse? Obviously, the gods had decided that Ben must pay for all his sins in one twenty-four-hour period.

Was it not enough that upon entering the private parlor he had hired at the inn for himself, his current mistress, and her cousin, Ben had discovered a partially disrobed Blanche sitting on George Atwater's lap, their lips locked together in a most uncousinly kiss? If that was not sufficient retribution, surely overturning the rented gig, being thrown into the road, and hitting his forehead against the iron wheel should count for something. And now, after being lost in the driving snow for hours, and not reaching his new home until the wee hours, he must deal with some unhinged woman.

Finding the phosphorous box, Ben removed one of the short, wooden spills, dipped it into the little oxide-lined bottle, then pulled it quickly through the narrow bottle neck. The moment it met the air, the oxide-coated spill burst into flame.

Once he had touched the spill to the wick, Ben lifted the candlestick, then padded barefoot around the end of the bed. Stopping just in front of the dressing room, he held the candlestick aloft so that it cast a faint yellowish light onto the dark wood of the floor. "Now, madam," he said, "perhaps you would be so kind as to tell me the purpose for that Cheltenham drama you enacted."

The woman did not reply to his question. Instead, she stepped back out of the light, as though he had threatened her, and hid behind the dividing wall. The only sound was the soft ticking of the clock on the desk, and after muttering an oath, Ben attempted to curb his anger. "Had I climbed unexpectedly into *your* bed, Miss Whoever-you-are, I could readily understand such a display of maidenly virtue. As it happens, I had it on good authority that this particular room, and most especially this bed, was mine."

Actually, it had not been good authority, or even reasonably good authority. The drunken lout who had finally answered the knocker could do nothing but mumble repeatedly about a "fancy," and the ashen-faced female who introduced herself as the housekeeper did nothing but bob curtsies and beg Ben to excuse her husband if he had done something he should not have.

Due to the growing list of unpleasant events that had befallen Ben that day, he had been in no mood to deal with either the lout or the housekeeper. He had but one wish: to climb into bed and hope his aching head would be better by morning. To that end, he took the candle the lout held, told the man to see to the hired gig and horse, then told the housekeeper he meant to sleep late, and that he was not to be disturbed until he rang for his breakfast.

Now, as Ben thought about it, it was quite possible that under those circumstances he had come to the

wrong room. It had been years since he had been at
Holden House; perhaps this was not the master bedchamber.

There was still no comment from the female hiding
behind the wall.

"Well?" he said. "This is my bedchamber, is it not?"

Ben took her continued silence for an affirmative
answer.

"Speak up, madam. You made enough noise a few
moments ago. In fact, my poor head is pounding
yet, so unless you wish me to come in there and pull
you out, I advise you to tell me who you are and what
you are doing here."

For several seconds all was quiet, save for the clock
chiming the half hour, and Ben began to suspect that he
would, indeed, be obliged to remove the woman by
force. To his relief, she made such action unnecessary by
stepping into the pool of light, her head bowed. Her
brown hair had once been secured in a knot atop her
head, but as a result of their tussle, at least half of the
thick tresses now hung free, obscuring her face.

He saw only a bit of her chin. However, because she
wore almost no clothing—nothing more than thin cot-
ton drawers and an even thinner lawn shift—Ben got
a pretty good look at the rest of her. Obviously unable
to find her discarded clothes in the dark, she now attempted to hide behind a long, narrow, knitted scarf.
Understandably, the scarf did not cover much.

Ben took his time looking her over. She was slender,
with well-turned ankles and long, rather shapely legs.
Her waist was trim and her hips were gently
rounded, but the rest of her was hidden behind the
scarf she clutched to her chest. Not that it mattered,
for after tussling with her, Ben had a pretty good idea
of the size and shape of her breasts.

Though her figure was appealing, at the moment it
was her face he wanted to see. "Look up," he ordered.

Whether from reticence or stubbornness, she took her own sweet time about obeying him. Ben had begun to think he would be obliged to repeat his order when she finally pushed the obscuring hair back over her shoulder and lifted her face, looking him directly in the eyes, all but daring him to issue another command.

At his first real look at her, he felt the breath knocked from his lungs. *Phoebe!*

No! It was a mistake. A trick of the light. It had to be.

The injury to his head had obviously addled his brain; there could be no other reason for his thinking this woman was Phoebe Lowell. She was not, of course. Such a thing was impossible. What the devil would Phoebe be doing here in his house? In his bed!

Instinctively, Ben reached out and caught the woman's chin, and though she tried to resist, he held her fast. Lifting the candle so it shone upon her face, he turned her head first one way and then the other, unable to credit how much she resembled Phoebe.

She was older than Phoebe, of course, well past her first blush of youth, and where Phoebe had possessed a young girl's petal-soft cheeks, this woman's face was leaner, sculptured by maturity. The cheekbones were more pronounced, and the chin was decidedly stubborn. She was handsome enough, but she lacked Phoebe's fresh-faced beauty.

"Who are you?" he demanded. "And what are you doing here?"

When he asked who she was, something showed in her eyes. Was it relief? Regret? Whatever it was, she chose not to answer his questions. Instead, she slapped at his wrist, pulling her chin free of his restraining hand. "I will not be interrogated," she said, "by a man who is . . . is *en déshabillé.*"

En déshabillé! Now there was an old-maidish turn of phrase. Ben was naked and they both knew it, and from her dogged effort to keep her gaze fixed firmly on his face, she was far more discomforted by his lack of clothing than he was. Good. Why should he be the only one to suffer?

And he was suffering. He had been from the moment she spoke the first few words.

At the sound of her voice, Ben had felt as though someone had hit him in the solar plexus with a battering ram; hit him, then left him lying in the road, raw and bleeding. Seven plus years and poor lighting might cause him not to recognize the face, but the voice was unmistakable. It was exactly the same, and it belonged to Phoebe Lowell . . . to the woman who had once held his heart in her hands. Held it, then dashed it into a million pieces.

She was talking, Ben could see her lips move, but he had no idea what she was saying. He felt numb all over, and he seemed unable to focus. "What is it?" he asked. "What did you say?"

"I said cover yourself!"

Still unnerved by the realization that Phoebe Lowell was in his bedchamber, wearing nothing but thin lawn underpinnings, he walked over to where he had dropped his clothes earlier and retrieved his breeches. After stepping into the damp kerseymere and fastening the fall, he returned to Phoebe. She stood where he had left her, although she had turned her back while he dressed.

"If you will give me the candle," she said, "so I can find my clothes, I will be out of your way in a matter of minutes."

"Did I say you were in my way?"

"No, but—"

"Then do not put words in my mouth."

"All the same, I should like to get dressed."

For the first time, Ben noticed that she was shivering. "Here," he said, pulling one of the blankets from the bed and holding it out to her, "wrap yourself in this, then sit over there by the desk. You still have not answered my questions."

She took the blanket and wrapped it around her, but she did not move toward the chair.

"Sit down," he said again. "It is not a request."

"I did not think it was."

When she still did not move, Ben swore. "Do it of your own volition, madam, or I will carry you. Either way, you are not leaving this room until I get some answers."

After giving him a look that left him in no doubt of her displeasure, she crossed to the desk and perched, stiff-backed, on the edge of the wooden chair. While she tucked her bare feet beneath the ends of the blanket, Ben lit all six candles in the cobalt blue candelabra and moved it within inches of her. He wanted to see her face while she answered his questions.

"I was caught off guard by the storm," she began without prompting, "so I sought shelter here. Had there been any other place to go, I would have done so."

He noticed that she ignored the question regarding her name. Fine. They would see which one of them could pretend the longest that they were unacquainted.

"I had injured my knee," she continued, "and I feared I could not walk the three miles back to Coalport before nightfall."

"Coalport? Where is that?"

"North of here. Just across Iron Bridge. On the other side of the River Severn."

"Are you visiting friends there?"

She shook her head. "I live there." Color stained her cheeks, but when she spoke again, her chin jutted out defiantly. "I am employed at the pottery factory, as a china painter."

Pottery factory! Did she take him for a fool? Why

would Phoebe Lowell be employed at all? Especially in such a place? Sir Lawrence was as starched up as they come, filled with pride in his family's name. He would never allow his only relative to associate with factory workers.

"Where is your family?" Ben asked. "Where is your . . ." He had meant to ask after her uncle, but he stopped himself just in time. ". . . your husband?"

The question surprised him as much as it apparently did her, for this time her cheeks showed more than a hint of color.

"I have no family," she replied, "and I am unmarried."

Unmarried? Was she a widow?

As if in answer to the question he did not ask, she said, "I am a spinster. I am not now, nor have I ever been married."

Ben found that almost impossible to believe. At nineteen, Phoebe Lowell had been the prettiest girl at Almack's, and the object of more than one man's admiration. Before he could ask her why she was not wed, however, she stood and picked up the single candle. "Now, my lord, you know all there is to know of me, and I should like to get dressed. Mrs. Curdy will be wondering why I have not returned."

My lord? She had used his title. So, Phoebe knew he was the new baron. If she knew that, it meant she knew as well that this was his house.

"Mrs. Curdy?" he said, choosing to ignore all else for the moment. "And she is?"

"My landlady. I live in a female dormitory for unmarried factory workers."

In the light from the candles, Ben could see Phoebe's expression; it was as haughty as a queen's, all but daring him to make some disparaging remark. Still, something in her voice convinced him that she spoke the truth about living in a dormitory, and he was human enough to gloat just a bit.

My, how the mighty have fallen!

Phoebe Lowell had refused his proposal of marriage—an honorable proposal—and now she was alone in the world. She was a hireling, obliged to earn her daily bread and share her living quarters with her coworkers, when she might have been Lady Holden, mistress of Holden House.

Was that her reason for being here? To see if she could recoup her losses? Was her objective to try her hand at rekindling the love she had spurned all those years ago? There was, after all, a prosperous estate as well as a title at stake now, and Phoebe would not be the first female to have a go at bringing the new Lord Holden up to scratch.

A sudden thought occurred to Ben, causing him to bite back an obscenity. If his head had not been pounding so when that poor excuse for a servant had let him into the house, Ben would have realized what the drunken lout was mumbling. Ben had thought the fellow had said, "Your fancy," when what he had actually said was, "Your fiancée."

Damnation! Phoebe had gained entrance to the house by passing herself off as Ben's fiancée.

What nerve! What unmitigated gall!

Phoebe Lowell had broken his heart—shattered his youthful illusions of love and fidelity—and now here she was trying to insinuate herself back into his life. And she had the audacity to call herself his fiancée, as if she had accepted his proposal all those years ago and had been waiting faithfully for his return so they could be married.

She would definitely catch cold on that!

If marriage was her objective, then she had badly misjudged her man. And Ben was not above showing her just how mistaken she was. In fact, he might enjoy doing just that.

As he stood there, looking at her wrapped in the faded counterpane from the bed, her shoulders back and her head held high, as though she wore the robes of a queen, an idea began to take hold in his brain. An idea that would not be denied.

Here was the woman who had played fast and loose with his emotions; encouraging him one moment, then rejecting him out of hand the following day. Without a qualm, she had trampled on his offer of lifelong devotion, and Ben owed it to himself to show her the error of her ways. Let her get her hopes up this time, perhaps even fall in love with him. After all, turnabout was fair play. And this time, Miss Phoebe Lowell would learn how it felt to be told she did not measure up to *his* standards.

"If you were the last man on earth," she had said that day in May, almost eight years ago, *"I would not consent to marry you."*

Ben had loved Phoebe with all his heart, had loved her with a passion that blinded him to all other females; and yet, his beloved had accused him of being a rake, a known seducer of women. At that time, nothing could have been further from the truth, for though Ben was twenty-three, he was only slightly more experienced than the nineteen-year-old Phoebe.

Eight years ago, Ben Holden had been a naive young soldier, but the same could not be said of him today. Though *he* did not consider himself a rake, he doubted there were many who would agree with him. Certainly he was not a rake in the strictest sense of the word, having always drawn the line at stealing the hearts of innocent damsels.

Naturally, when it came to the more worldly ladies, Ben seldom refused what was offered. Women liked him and he liked women, and he knew to a nicety how to please them. He knew what made them purr. Of course, he had always been scrupulously truthful with his paramours, never leading them to believe that the liaison was anything more than a temporary arrangement.

If Ben was the one to end the affair, he always left his *chère amies* pretty parting gifts that more than dried any tears. And if the women were first to bid him *adieu*, at least none of them had ever broken his heart. Not the way Phoebe had. It had taken him years to get over the pain of losing her.

Phoebe had said she loved him, had led him to believe she wanted to spend her life with him, and yet she had thrown him over on the flimsiest of evidence of wrongdoing. She had taken the word of one person, when she should have loved Ben enough to trust in him. He had trusted in her.

Unfortunately, she had not deserved his trust.

And now, what she deserved was a bit of her own back.

Nothing serious, of course; nothing like the heartbreak she had caused him. Just a little payback for not believing in him. And perhaps an added measure for having the nerve to think she could get away with passing herself off as his fiancée. This time, let Phoebe shed a few tears over losing him.

First, though, Ben would have to make her believe that he still loved her, and he would have to make her fall in love with him again. Fortunately, that should not prove too difficult. Ben was no longer a gullible young man still wet behind the ears. He was a skillful lover, and he knew where women were most vulnerable. He should have no trouble discovering the chinks in Miss Phoebe Lowell's armor.

All he had to do was keep her here at Holden House long enough to do the job.

Chapter Four

After leaving the bedroom, Phoebe remained in the dressing room for fully fifteen minutes, though it had taken her no more than five of those minutes to don her petticoat, her dress, and her stockings. Her boots were still damp, and the leather was cold to the touch, but all too aware that what could not be helped must be endured, Phoebe stepped into the stiff boots and pulled them up over her ankles.

Once she was dressed, she sat in the barber chair and stared at the guttering candle. She heard the clock on the desk chime six times, but try as she might, she could not get up the nerve to go back into the bedchamber. Ben Holden was in there, perhaps still barechested, and though he did not seem to recognize her—a fact for which she offered up a prayer of thanksgiving—she found it much too embarrassing to be in the same room with him.

If she lived to be a hundred years old, none of those future birthdays could possibly top this one for unallayed mortification. Apparently, the fates were having a little joke at her expense. Otherwise, how had she wound up in Ben's bed, pressed against his naked body?

A shiver ran through her at the remembered warmth of his skin, and the solid feel of his muscular arm pulling her close. "Do not think about it," she muttered. "Put it from your mind as though it were really the dream you believed it to be."

This was not the way her first meeting with the new Lord Holden was supposed to go. Apparently, the Scottish poet, Mr. Robert Burns, was in the right of it when he wrote that the best laid plans of mice and men often went astray.

From the moment Phoebe had realized the true identity of the new master of Holden House, she had played a scenario over and over in her mind—a scenario in which she avoided seeing Ben Holden for as long as possible. In her imagination, their initial meeting would be by chance, probably in the village, and each time she imagined that encounter, it was always at some unspecified time in the distant future.

Ha! Like so many of her plans, that one had "gang" astray with a vengeance. Avoid Ben? Somehow she had managed to be the first person to greet him. And wearing nothing but a shift and drawers!

Could the situation be any worse?

Of course, it could be worse, and Phoebe's stomach pitched unpleasantly just thinking of the fabrication that would exacerbate the situation. To her relief, Ben had not recognized her in the dim light. Eventually, though, he would discover her identity, and he would find out as well that she had gained entrance to his house by posing as his fiancée. And Phoebe did not want to be here when he learned the truth.

Ben would think she had come around to have a go at becoming Lady Holden, and in light of their past, he would be livid. Justifiably so. The thought of his anger was enough to spur Phoebe to action.

If she made a dash for it, there was a good chance she could make it to the bedchamber door and down the stairs before Ben realized her intention. When she had sought refuge in the house, she meant to remain only until daylight, and the clock had already sounded six. If it was not light now, it would be soon.

Resolved to escape, Phoebe gathered up her scarf and her cloak, blew out the candle, then peeped around the wall to see if Ben was between her and the bedchamber door. He was not. He had lighted the fire, and already its warmth was reaching to the far corners of the bedchamber. Ben had also blown out the candles on the desk, but the flames from the fireplace cast a soft glow over the room, supplying sufficient light to show Phoebe that the coast was clear.

Ben must have gotten back under the covers to keep warm. Good. Phoebe would not be obliged to push her way past him. Grateful to have escaped another embarrassing scene, she tiptoed across the turkey carpet, all the while keeping her gaze on the bed, lest Ben leap forward suddenly and try to bar her way. Being as quiet as possible, she turned the handle and opened the door, and to her relief, no one rushed forward to stop her.

Phoebe did not bother closing the door. She merely fled down the corridor, happy to be away from Ben Holden. Lifting the hem of her skirt so it did not trip her, she hurried past the other four bedchambers and down the marble stairs to the vestibule. Unfortunately, when she arrived at the heavy entrance doors, she found them bolted shut.

The iron latch was thick and in need of lubrication, and for a minute Phoebe thought she would be unable to free it from the equally stubborn sheath. Unwilling to admit defeat, she pounded the cylinder several times with the heel of her hand, then attempted to pull the bolt free once again. This time it gave way, and she was able to pull it back.

She delayed her departure only long enough to throw her cloak around her shoulders and fasten the frog at her neck. In her haste to be belowstairs, she had lost her scarf, but she dared not go back to search for it. Never mind; she could knit herself another scarf. What mattered now was getting out of Holden House before Ben discovered who she was and the lie she had told.

As luck would have it, the moment she swung wide the heavy front door, Phoebe realized that leaving Holden House was impossible. The wind had ceased to howl, the snow had stopped falling, and there were signs of light in the sky; unfortunately, the snow that lay on the ground was at least three feet deep. As well, the air was so cold that when Phoebe drew a breath, it burned deep inside her lungs, all but choking her.

Cupping her hands over her mouth and nose to protect them from the cold, Phoebe stared at the freshly fallen snow banked against the distant trees. The drifts were a good six feet deep, and she could not even find the carriageway. No matter how compelling her reasons for wanting to escape, there was no way she could walk through snow that deep.

Phoebe had told Ben that Mrs. Curdy would be wondering what had happened to her, but even if that were true, no search party would come out to look for her today. Not in weather this cold. Any sensible person would know that if Phoebe had spent the night out-of-doors, she would be frozen by now, and buried beneath feet of snow, well beyond the help of a rescue party. On the other hand, if she had taken refuge in someone's house or barn, it stood to reason that she would be better off remaining where she was until the temperature rose at least thirty degrees.

Since no party of concerned villagers would be searching for Phoebe Lowell, china painter—not today at least—and since Pheobe was not foolish enough to try to reach Coalport on her own, there was no hope for it. She must remain at Holden House. Resigned to her fate, she closed the door and shot the bolt.

What she was to do here, she could not even guess, but one thing was certain, she could not go back upstairs. That left her with no option but to make her way to one of the two rooms she had noticed yesterday. Once there, she would find a settee, curl up on it, and tuck her cloak around her for warmth. And there she would remain until someone found her and told her to get out.

After staring at the whiteness of the snow, the vestibule seemed doubly dark, and Phoebe was obliged to run her hand along the circular wall, feeling her way to the archway that gave access to the room on the left. Due to its location near the front door, she assumed the room was used as an informal reception area. If that was the case, however, the reception would need to be very informal, for the room was completely bare. To Phoebe's amazement, there was not one stick of furniture, though she could have sworn she remembered seeing a couple of pieces beneath Holland covers.

Assuming she was confused—after all, she had rushed through here yesterday—Phoebe crossed the vestibule to the room on the right. Paneled in a dark wood of some kind, and with no rug on the floor, the room echoed with the sound of her footfalls, for this space, too, was empty. No chairs, no tables, no settees, and not a sign of the Holland covers.

How bizarre! Yesterday Phoebe had seen furniture in one of these rooms, and the evidence to the contrary, she knew she had not been mistaken.

As if needing to touch something that would not disappear before her eyes, Phoebe crossed to the fireplace and put both hands on the gray slate mantel. The stone was thick with dust, and cold to the touch, and as Phoebe withdrew her hands and brushed them together to remove the grit from her fingertips, she heard a loud thumping noise behind the wall just to the left of the fireplace.

Startled, she gasped, then moved back several feet.

The thump, which sounded as if something had bumped against the wall from the inside, was followed by a sort of scratching noise. Mice? There were mice in the attic at Mrs. Curdy's, and at night, when the house was quiet, Phoebe often heard the rodents chewing their way down the inside of the walls.

Naturally, she was not the sort of pampered widgeon who screamed at the sight of a mouse, but she had never heard anything to match the noise coming from behind those panels. If that was mice back there, they must be the size of house cats, and Phoebe wanted no part of them!

She exited the room at a quick walk, but by the time she reached the bottom stair, her speed had increased to a run. She did not even slow down until she was on the next floor. After stopping to catch her breath at the top of the stairs, Phoebe looked down the corridor toward the master bedchamber. The door she had not bothered to close when she fled the room was still open, and lying just over the threshold, almost as if someone had placed it there, was her missing scarf.

Not that Phoebe had any plans to retrieve the item. A thousand scarves, all of them made of the purest silk, would not tempt her to go down that corridor!

Here was a fine mess. She could not leave the house; she was frightened to remain belowstairs; and a half-naked man awaited her abovestairs. And not just any half-naked man, but one who had every reason to despise her.

Phoebe was leaning against the newel post, wondering what she should do, and wishing she still believed in answered prayers, when she heard a moan. Certain the sound had come from the master bedchamber, she tiptoed to the door and peeped inside the room. It looked just as it had when she left it several minutes ago, with the fire still crackling invitingly, and Ben nowhere to be seen.

She was about to pick up her scarf and return to the corridor when she heard a second moan. The sound came from somewhere inside the massive bed, and unless Phoebe was mistaken, the moaner was in real distress.

Earlier, when Phoebe was still in that bed, pinned beneath Ben's restraining arm and leg, he had said something about being injured. At the time, Phoebe had thought he was merely making sport of her, but perhaps he had spoken the truth. Perhaps he was hurt.

A third moan, slightly louder than the first two, convinced her that Ben was suffering.

Still embarrassed by all that had passed between them earlier, Phoebe walked rather hesitantly to the foot of the bed. Ben was there, with the covers pulled up neatly to his waist. He was sitting up, propped against a bank of pillows supported by the carved, ebony headboard. His head was laid back, and he had placed his left arm across his eyes, as if to shield them from the light of the fire.

To Phoebe's relief, he had donned a white linen shirt. Unfortunately, the neck of the shirt gaped open, and she was momentarily distracted by the sight of Ben's broad chest and the liberal sprinkling of short, silky hair that curled at the base of his throat—hair as dark a brown as that on his head. But at least he was covered!

"Ohhh," he moaned again, though so softly Phoebe only just heard it.

On the instant, her embarrassment vanished, lost in the concern any human being would feel for someone who was in pain. "What is amiss?" she asked, taking several steps closer to the man in the bed. "Are you ill, my lord?"

"No," he said softly, his face still partially concealed behind his arm. "At least nothing to signify."

"Can I be of help?"

"Would that you could, ma'am. Unfortunately, no one can help me. But do not, I beg of you, worry on my account. I am persuaded I shall be better by morning. Or at least by the following day. The pain seldom lasts more than a few days."

Seldom lasts?

Recalling the rumor that Ben had been wounded while serving in the Peninsula, and that his wound had been serious enough to send him home to England to recuperate, Phoebe approached his bedside and gently removed his arm from over his closed eyes. "Please," she said, "allow me to see if you have a fever."

When Ben voiced no objections, Phoebe placed the back of her hand upon his forehead. His brow was slightly warm, though not dangerously so. "I am persuaded you have no fever, sir. However, if you should like—"

"Try here," he murmured, gently capturing her hand and turning it over so that her palm lay against the side of his angular face.

It was all Phoebe could do not to snatch her hand away, for at the touch of Ben's strong fingers upon her wrist, she had felt her own skin grow unnaturally warm. After a moment, however, she managed to speak. "Cool there as well, my lord."

"And here?" he asked, sliding her palm downward past his square, rather determined jaw, then still farther down to the wide, strong column of his throat.

Phoebe had never touched a man's neck before, and when the tip of her little finger accidentally dipped inside the opening of Ben's shirt and encountered several of those silky hairs she had seen earlier, heat raced from her fingertips all the way to her toes.

"Well?" Ben whispered.

The sound of that one, softly spoken word, combined with the heat that was invading every inch of Phoebe's body, had a mesmerizing effect upon her, causing her to sway ever so slightly toward the bed. Almost as if *she* had somehow contracted a fever.

Her hand was still on Ben's neck when he swallowed . . . once . . . twice . . . three times, and with each swallow, his Adam's apple eased up and down slowly against Phoebe's palm. The movement was like nothing she had ever felt before, and it caused a tingling sensation inside her midsection—a tingling that slowly spread to other parts of her body.

A pulse began to throb in her wrist, its rhythm further mesmerizing her, and Phoebe had the strangest desire to move her hand down even lower, so it rested against Ben's heart. She might have given in to the temptation if a sudden gust of wind had not rattled the windows as if bent on shaking the glass free of the frames.

The spell broken—and spell it must have been—Phoebe jumped back, well out of temptation's reach, all the while taking herself to task for acting like the veriest ninnyhammer merely because she had touched a man. "N-no fever," she said. "Even so, a cool compress might make you feel better."

"You are very kind, ma'am, but nothing can make me feel better. There is no panacea for a man whose pain is more mental than physical."

Ben opened his eyes just enough to get a look at Phoebe's face. It was as he suspected, her color was high and her breathing shallow. She was twenty-seven-years old, a woman grown, but unless Ben missed his guess, she was as inexperienced today as she had been eight years ago.

Not that it changed his plan. Not in any appreciable way. He still meant to have his revenge upon her; only now that he knew she was a novice at the art of love, he would need to move more slowly. It would not do to frighten her into seeking help from the housekeeper, thereby gaining for herself a chaperone. Once the weather cleared, and Phoebe left Holden House, Ben might never have her in his power again.

When she had fled the bedchamber, Ben followed her to the top of the staircase, where he watched her struggle with the stubborn latch. He said nothing, merely waited to see what would happen. She had finally managed to open the front door, but she had not stepped outside. Ben was not surprised.

He had been out there not too many hours ago, so the deep snow came as no revelation to him, nor did the bitter cold that rushed into the vestibule and up the stairs, making his bare feet feel like blocks of ice. He needed no reminder of that freezing air to help him understand why his uninvited guest had stood unmoving in the doorway.

Whatever she was, Phoebe Lowell was not stupid. Certain death awaited anyone foolish enough to go outside in this weather, and if the previous month was anything to judge by, the situation would not change for days to come. January had been bitterly cold, with the Thames freezing over for more than a week, and so far February looked like it might prove even more inclement than its predecessor.

When Phoebe closed the door and shot home the bolt, Ben smiled. Moments later, he had crept back to the bedchamber, confident that in time Phoebe would return there as well, if only to keep warm.

His assumption had been correct, and now he had her where he wanted her—in his room, touching him, and reacting to that touch. It was a good start.

"Ohh," he moaned, and instantly Phoebe was beside him again, her gray eyes filled with concern.

"Lord Holden, if there is anything I can do to relieve your distress, be it mental or physical, you have only to tell me. Whatever it entails, rest assured I will do it."

Ben sighed dramatically. "If only you could, ma'am. When I first saw you, I thought you might be my savior—the answer to my prayers, but then— No," he said, turning his face away from her, "I cannot burden you with my problems."

Slowly, tentatively she reached out and put one finger beneath his chin, then gently turned his face back toward her. "I cannot think, sir, that I am the answer to anyone's prayers, but I wish you would tell me why you thought I might be."

Ben did not reply right away, merely gazing into her eyes, letting the drama of silence pique her curiosity, luring her like a trout in a stream. Finally, when he was certain his fish was sufficiently curious not to bolt at his first words, he said, "There is something about you, ma'am, something vaguely familiar."

Her eyes widened in surprise, but before she could become frightened, he jiggled the bait once more. "I had hoped—nay, I had prayed—that you might have known me before . . . before a Frenchman's bullet stole my life from me."

"Stole your life? But, sir, you are alive."

"Only partially. I tell you, ma'am, when a man is robbed of all his dearest memories, even the recollection of his own name, he might as well be dead."

She stared at him, incredulity written upon her face. "Are you telling me, my lord, that you have no memory? None whatsoever?"

"No. It is not quite as bad as that. I remember all that has transpired during this past year. Unfortunately, everything that happened to me before the injury is a blank. It is as if my life never happened. As if the people I knew—the people I loved for the first twenty-nine years of my existence—were wiped forever from my mind."

He sighed again. "I have no recollection of my childhood, of my school years, or of my early days as a soldier. As for my friends and family, they might as well never have been born. Why, the physicians had to tell me my own name."

"Oh, no."

"Oh, yes. And with that I discovered the one thing that gives me hope."

He paused, allowing his little trout time to spot the lure once again.

"What is it that gives you hope, sir?"

"To my great joy, madam, I discovered that once I am told something of my past, it returns to me, almost as if I had remembered it myself. You cannot know what that means to me. With each new memory, it is as if I am healed, one small piece at a time. As if I am brought back to life, one meager fact at a time. Only . . ."

"Only?" she prompted.

"Only there are too few people who knew me before I was injured. Fellow officers have filled in much of my army experiences, but to my infinite regret, there is no one—none but mere acquaintances, I should say—who knew me prior to those war years. I have prayed for such a person, for someone who knew me even a little, but so far my prayers have gone unanswered."

While he talked, Ben had watched Phoebe's eyes, for they revealed the battle being waged inside her—a battle between sympathy and caution. She was genuinely sympathetic, he was forced to admit that much, and she appeared sincere in her offer to help him. And yet, she obviously did not wish to remind him of their past association. And why should she? If she cherished hopes of bringing him up to scratch, of getting him to propose to her again, it was not in her best interest to remind him of the day she had refused him.

She had remained beside the bed, and now Ben reached out and caught her hand in his. "Forgive me, Miss . . ." He paused, offering her an opportunity to fill in the name.

"Lowell," she said. "Phoebe Lowell."

"Forgive me, Miss Lowell, for burdening you with my personal tragedy. And you a perfect stranger. It is just that I had hoped . . . No! I must not say it. I must stop hoping, and learn to be grateful for what memories I have."

Phoebe's throat felt tight with unshed tears. Poor Ben. Poor, gallant Ben. His bravery shamed her. After years of fighting Napoleon's soldiers, Ben had been grievously injured in the defense of his country, and he had prayed for but one thing—someone who might tell him something of the life he had forgotten.

For the past hour, Phoebe had been thinking only of her own discomfort, afraid Ben would remember that they had once been engaged. What a selfish person she had become! Guilty of unabashed egotism, she tried to make amends. "What is it, my lord, that you feel you must not say?"

"I must not tell you, Miss Lowell, how my heart soared when I first beheld your face and thought that you looked familiar. It was foolish of me, I know, especially in this remote place, to think I might meet an old acquaintance. Still, when I saw you, I was persuaded the gods had smiled upon me at last, and at the prospect of discovering a little more of my past— no matter how insignificant the facts might seem to the teller—I was hard pressed not to weep."

With that, he cleared his throat, as if to forestall the

threatening tears. "I apologize, ma'am, for this display of emotion."

Phoebe was obliged to clear her own throat. "Actually, sir, it is I who should apologize."

"You, Miss Lowell? Whatever for? What sins have you committed?"

"Many, I assure you, my lord, but the sin for which I must ask your pardon is one of omission. When you thought there was something vaguely familiar about me, you . . . you were not mistaken."

"We are acquainted? Why did you not say something right away?"

Phoebe had the grace to blush. "We met in the spring, eight years ago, in London. But," she hurried to add, "we knew one another for only a matter of weeks. At that time you were a young lieutenant, not Lord Holden, and now that you have succeeded to the title, and are master of Holden House, I did not want you to think I meant to presume upon such a brief acquaintance."

Ben waved his hand as if to dismiss such a foolish notion, then he bid Phoebe take off her cloak and pull the Windsor chair close to the fire, so she might be comfortable. When she complied, he said, "I can scarce believe my good fortune. Would you be willing to share some of your memories with me, Miss Lowell? To help me recall our friendship? How it began, and how it grew. All of it."

She studied her hands, the fingers linked together as if to keep them from trembling. "Actually, my lord, there is little to tell."

"There is little to tell?" Ben asked, an unbidden hint of bitterness creeping into his voice, "or little that you wish to tell?"

She looked up at him suddenly, uncertainty in her eyes. Fearing he had gone too far, Ben forced himself to speak calmly. "A few minutes ago you tried to run away. Was that because our friendship did not end amicably? You may be brutally frank with me, ma'am. Did I do something to give you a disgust of me? Something you hold against me still?"

"To the contrary, my lord. It is I who feared that you might hold me in dislike."

"Never! Whatever happened, Miss Lowell, whatever it was, I am persuaded there must have been a good reason for it." He looked deeply into her eyes. "Forget the thing that came between us, and tell me only of the good things.

"And whatever you do, Miss Lowell, do not feel you must escape this house. Until such time as you may safely return to Coalport, consider yourself an honored guest."

Though Phoebe's cheeks turned pink, she appeared to relax. "Thank you, my lord."

"So," Ben said, offering her his hand, "do we have a bargain? Will you remain here until the weather improves? And will you agree to be my Scheherazade?"

Phoebe had started to place her hand in his, but at his last question, she hesitated. "Scheherazade? Is she not the Persian maiden who married the sultan, only to discover that he made a practice of strangling his wives the morning after the wedding?"

Drat! He had forgotten how quick Phoebe was. "I believe that version of the story is generally held to be true. Legend has it, however, that the newest bride was no fool. A clever girl, she ensured her life by telling the sultan a story each evening, keeping him entertained for a thousand and one nights. But have no fear, Miss Lowell, I have no plans to strangle you."

Phoebe smiled, albeit hesitantly. "I am relieved to hear it, my lord."

Ben offered his hand once again. "Come, madam, have we a bargain? You cannot mean to cry craven, not now. Not after inspiring me to hope that I might get back a bit of what I lost."

Phoebe placed her hand in his, but she left it there for only a matter of seconds. "I will not cry craven," she said softly.

"My brave Scheherazade," Ben said, bestowing upon Phoebe a smile one of his paramours had once described as being disarming enough to trick the devil. "You cannot begin to imagine what it means to me to have you here."

"I . . . I hope, sir, that you will not be disappointed."

"Never," Ben said, then he lowered his gaze, lest she read his true meaning in his eyes. "I am persuaded, ma'am, that this will be a reunion neither of us will ever forget."

Chapter Five

Scheherazade. Phoebe was obliged to force back a nervous giggle. As she sat beside the fire, all too aware of her worn boots and her old blue merino dress, which was stained with snow and wrinkled beyond belief, she wondered if there could be anyone less like the heroine of an exotic Persian story. And yet, she had given Ben her promise, and she would not go back on her word.

She was uncertain where to begin her reminiscences, and even less certain how to avoid mentioning the last day she had ever seen Ben—the day she had accused him of being a rake. As it turned out, she need not have worried, for Ben started the ball rolling by asking her questions about her job as china painter at the pottery factory.

As she answered his queries, Phoebe strove to make her present life appear pleasant, even going so far as to joke about one of the girls who shared her room at Mrs. Curdy's. "Until that first night," she said, "I did not know that females snored."

Ben smiled. "I have no doubt that many ladies snore, but should they be guilty of such an egregious fault, I cannot think they would admit to it."

"I know I would not," Phoebe said. "In any event, I had no idea, not until I was awakened that first night, unable to discern the origin of the terrible noise emanating from the far side of the room. The sound alternated between a deep buzzing and a sort of high-pitched whirring, and after listening to it for some ten minutes, I decided that a swarm of angry bees had invaded our small bedchamber."

Ben chuckled, and encouraged, Phoebe continued with her story. "You will think me the veriest looby, sir, for I spent the remainder of the night shivering with fear, my head hidden beneath the cover, awaiting the apian attack."

"You did not."

"I vow, 'tis true. And you may imagine my dismay when the sun rose and I discovered there were no bees to be found. Only poor Irma, lying on her back, her mouth hanging open, snoring fit to burst our eardrums."

Ben laughed appreciatively, but after a minute or two of listening to a description of the village, he asked if she would forgive him if he closed his eyes for a time. "Just for a short nap."

Having forgotten that he had said his head hurt, Phoebe rose from the chair, apologizing profusely.

"Do not be concerned," he said. "I will be better after some sleep. In the meanwhile, Miss Lowell, please stay beside the fire where you may be comfortable. If the drunken lout who greeted me at the door is indicative of the servants here, I suspect this house is unfit for visitors. Later, after I have rested a bit, I will have a talk with the housekeeper and make certain that you are provided with a suitable bedchamber."

"Thank you, my lord."

"Please," he said, "if we were once friends enough for you to call me by my name, I beg you will you give me that pleasure again."

"If that is your wish," she replied. "Thank you, Ben."

"Thank you, Scheherazade."

With that, Ben turned over on his side, and after pulling the covers up over his shoulders, he slept.

Phoebe remained in the Windsor chair until she was warm through and through. Once daylight spread to every corner of the bedchamber, she tiptoed to the dressing room, combed her fingers through her hair, then arranged it as best she could in its usual knot atop her head. Reasonably presentable, she decided to brave the area belowstairs once again. After all, if she was to remain at Holden House for what might prove to be days, she would be obliged to face the servants sooner or later.

Phoebe descended the wide, cantilevered stairs at a normal pace—a singular experience for her—noting as she did so the artistry of the builder of the seemingly floating staircase. The marble surface was still handsome, though the middle of each step showed slight indentations where a century's worth of feet had trod, and as Phoebe looked about her at the staircase and the vestibule, she acknowledged that with a little care this could be a very handsome establishment.

Behind the stairs, a narrow corridor led to the rear of the house, and Phoebe followed it, hoping she would eventually find something to eat and drink. As it happened, locating the kitchen was not difficult; Phoebe had only to follow her nose.

The Pied Piper's tunes could not have been any more enticing to the children of Hamlin than the aroma of a fresh-baked savory pudding was to Phoebe Lowell. She had not eaten so much as a morsel since her nuncheon at the gorge yesterday, and her stomach had begun to growl at least an hour ago. As well, she was in dire need of a glass of water.

She stopped at the threshold of a warm, cheery kitchen, pleased to note a well-scrubbed cobbled floor and an ancient, yet still sturdy, deal table. Two people sat at the long table, an aproned woman in her early forties and the servant who had opened the door last evening. The woman stared through the frost-covered windowpanes to the cold whiteness beyond, lost in thought, while the man sat with his elbows propped on the table, his face hidden in his hands. Apparently, neither of them had heard Phoebe approach.

"Do I smell coffee?" she asked.

The woman gasped, but the man, who looked up suddenly, groaned, grabbing his head as if it might fall off his shoulders at any moment. The fellow had shaved and donned a clean uniform, but no amount of cleanliness could conceal the fact that he was suffering from the results of having consumed an injudicious amount of home brew. His complexion had a decidedly pasty look, and from the pain revealed in his bloodshot eyes, he obviously thought he might die soon and wished only that the end would come quickly and put him out of his misery.

He groaned again, then resumed his earlier pose, with his face hidden in his hands, but the woman jumped to her feet and curtsied. "Forgive me, miss," she said, "but I did not hear the bell."

"I did not ring," she replied.

During the years following her uncle's death—years of near penury for Phoebe—she had forgotten there were such things as bell pulls in every room, and servants who appeared in answer to the rings. "Being unaware just how many servants were employed at the moment, I decided to come to the kitchen myself, to search for a cup of something warm to drink."

The woman made no reply to Phoebe's remark, merely crossed to an oak cupboard and removed a cup and saucer. Meanwhile, Phoebe studied her, recalling what the maid, Abby, had said about the housekeeper at Holden House being Mrs. Curdy's sister-in-law. It was difficult to believe those two could be related in any way. The woman must have been a beautiful young girl, for she was tall and slender, with hair the color of honey, and eyes a deep green.

She was still a handsome woman by anyone's standards. At least she might have been, if she had not appeared nervous enough to jump right out of her skin.

"Are you the housekeeper?" Phoebe asked.

"Yes, miss. I'm Mary Abbott, and over there is my husband."

The man rose from the bench, and after executing what Phoebe could only assume was meant for a bow, he made a hasty retreat through a door that must have led to the housekeeper's rooms.

"Abbott and me came to work for the previous Lord Holden two years ago," the woman said, as if to cover for her husband's lack of manners. "Just before his lordship's final illness."

"Are you two the only servants?"

"No, miss. There's a dairyman and a maid of all work, though she is new."

"Is that all? Just the four of you? For a house this large?"

If possible, the housekeeper appeared even more uncomfortable, though why that should be, Phoebe could not even guess. "The others. They . . . er, they left, miss."

Left? How curious. Reminding herself that what went on at Holden House was none of her affair, Phoebe asked no more questions.

Though Mary Abbott attempted to concentrate on the task of pouring coffee without sloshing it into the saucer, her gaze kept sliding nervously toward the deal table. Across the table from where she and her husband had been sitting were four empty plates, giving evidence that at least six people had recently broken their fasts.

Why this should occasion concern, Phoebe could not even guess. It was not as though Phoebe meant to report to the master that two extra people had been fed.

Whatever the cause for the housekeeper's agitation, Phoebe decided it could have nothing to do with her. Besides, she had concerns of her own.

In her usual naive way, she had started to introduce herself to Mary Abbott as one of Mrs. Curdy's boarders. Fortunately, Phoebe realized just in time what the consequences of such a revelation would be, so she clamped her lips together before they gave her away. She had told a falsehood to gain entrance to the house, and that had been all right when she thought she could quit the place before anyone got a good look at her.

Now, however, she was stuck here for who knew how long, and all she could think to do was continue with the fabrication. As well, she prayed that at some later date Mrs. Abbott would not pay a visit to her sister-in-law's house and find Phoebe sitting there with all the other factory workers.

If that happened, it would be Phoebe who would be answering the questions, and "uncomfortable" would not even begin to describe the way she would feel. Especially if it became known in Coalport that she had spent the night in Lord Holden's bed. Her reputation would be ruined, and getting the sack would be the least she could expect. And without her job, she would be destitute.

Hoping to bluff her way through this awkward situation, Phoebe employed the voice she might have once used with servants. "I am Miss Lowell," she said. After waiting for some word of acknowledgment from the housekeeper—acknowledgment that did not come—she pointed toward the end of the table, where no place had been laid. "Shall I sit there?"

The woman's mouth fell open in surprise, as if Phoebe had asked where she should begin demolishing the house. "At the table, miss? Here? In the kitchen?"

"Exactly."

Not waiting for approval, Phoebe seated herself upon the wooden stool. "It is my intention to break my fast, and though I have not explored the entire house, if there is another room in this establishment that boasts a warming fire, or so much as a stick of furniture, I have not found it."

At mention of the other rooms, Mrs. Abbott gasped, then she began to tremble, sloshing coffee all over the stone floor, and looking for all the world as if she might faint. Concerned, Phoebe rose to go to her, but before she had time to take more than a step, the housekeeper turned quickly, set the cup on the cupboard, then fled the room.

Deciding that the deplorable state of the house and the peculiar behavior of its servants were all of a piece, Phoebe retrieved her coffee and took it to the table. When her thirst was quenched, she found a fresh plate, served herself a more than ample portion of the savory pudding, then ate every morsel. Once her hunger had been satisfied, she poured herself another cup of coffee, using it as an excuse to linger at the table.

In time, however, the coffee gave out, as did Phoebe's justification for remaining in the kitchen. With no other option, she quit the warm room and returned to the chilly vestibule. The circular space was as empty as ever, so she sat on the bottom stair, her hands hidden in the folds of her skirt, and pondered her next move. She could sit there and grow cold once again or she could go back up to the master bedchamber. "Blast!" she muttered inelegantly. "Must it always be Hobson's choice with me?"

"Your pardon," said a frail, almost ghostly voice that seemed to come from nowhere. "Were you speaking to me?"

Phoebe turned quickly, looking all about her, searching the vestibule for any signs of human life; to her dismay, she found none. If she had been standing, her knees would have failed her. As it was, upon hearing that faint, disembodied voice, she felt gooseflesh pop out on the back of her neck.

Heaven help her! Was the house haunted?

Earlier, when she had heard the muffled noise behind the wall in the paneled room, she had told herself the sounds were made by mice. Not even in her worst nightmares, however, had mice ever spoken to her.

"I am a bit slow these days," the voice said, the words echoing as if uttered in some long-empty chamber. "Wait for me."

Wait! Not if my legs will carry me!

Phoebe turned, grabbed the bannister for support, and was pulling herself to her feet when the wall to her right, just at the beginning of the rear corridor, made a clicking noise, then swung open. Too frightened to speak, she stared at the apparition who stood just inside the opening. Female, small, and far from young, the specter wore a powdered wig whose one youthful screw curl rested against an elderly shoulder; her cheeks were rouged and powdered; and a tiny heart-shaped silk patch adorned the corner of her painted mouth. As well, she wore a moth-eaten ermine tippet over a green brocade dress that included the tightly laced bodice and the panniers in fashion half a century ago.

"Who are you?" the ghostlike creature said. "Have

you brought me a message? Is there a letter at last from my beloved Jamie?"

Phoebe swallowed, not yet certain if the odd-looking creature was still of this world or overdue in the next. "I . . . I brought no message," she finally managed to say.

Tears pooled in the apparition's eyes and spilled down her wrinkled cheeks, leaving salty tracks in the thick powder. "If you have no word for me from Jamie, then what are you doing in my house?" Not waiting for a reply, she added, "Go away. I am not receiving callers today."

Ben woke to find the anvil that had clanged inside his head since last evening had stilled at last. Only a slight ache remained, but since that was bearable, he felt he would soon be back to normal. Like most physically powerful men, he had little patience for illness, and was eager to be up and about.

He had no idea how long he had slept, but when he opened his eyes, the bedchamber was filled with daylight. Of Miss Phoebe Lowell, there was not a sign, but a young housemaid, complete with mobcap and starched apron, was on her knees before the hearth, replenishing the fire.

Before Ben could ask her where Phoebe was, he remembered the heavy snow and the fact that his guest was obliged to remain inside the house. Wherever she might be, there was time enough to find her later, after he was shaved and dressed.

"Good day," he said.

The startled maid, little more than a child, dropped the firewood she held, then tripped over it in her attempt to spring to her feet. "Oh, sir! " she said, bobbing an awkward curtsy, "you fair frightened me into an early grave."

"My apologies," Ben said. "I merely wished to

know if a hired chaise had arrived yet, for I am expecting my valet and my luggage."

The maid fixed her gaze on the basket of wood on the hearth, too embarrassed to look at her new employer. "I'm that sorry, my lord, but the chaise b'aint come. And no valet neither. Mayhap the storm held them up."

Ah, yes, the storm. Ben had been a fool to leave Fortson at the Tawny Lion. At the time, though, Ben had been too angry with himself for bringing his paramour to Shropshire, and too disgusted with Blanche, and with that scoundrel she had introduced as her cousin, to think clearly. Wanting nothing so much as to be relieved of the need to speak to that disreputable pair again, Ben had hired a gig for himself and left Fortson there at the inn with money enough to pay the shot, and instructions for the coachman to take the "cousins" back to London with all haste.

As for the valet, Ben had expected him to finish the distasteful business with Blanche, then continue to Holden House the next day with some hired conveyance and the luggage. Of course, Ben had not expected this wretched storm. No more than he had expected to find Phoebe Lowell again after all these years.

On second thought, perhaps it had all happened for the best. Fortson might queer Ben's scheme to have his revenge on Phoebe. The fellow had been batman to Ben the entire time they were in the Peninsula, and like most servants, he knew everything there was to know about his employer, including the fact that Ben had never suffered so much as a day's worth of amnesia.

The housemaid bobbed another curtsy. "If you was wondering what become of your coat and breeches, my lord, they be safe. I brushed 'em, like I was used to brush my grandfa's good coat, then I 'ung 'em in the dressing room. There be shirts aplenty in the clothespress, and other linens as well, enough for a dozen men, I be thinking. And while I were tidying up, I spied a leather box with a pair of razors inside. Ivory 'andled razors they be."

The girl obviously saw nothing amiss in Ben's making free with his deceased great-uncle's clothes, something Ben was loath to do, but he was glad to know about the razors. His beard grew quickly, and without the benefit of a good razor, he would soon resemble Father Christmas.

Apparently desirous of making a good impression, the girl continued with her helpful suggestions. "Shall I send Mr. Abbott up to your lordship? 'E's no gentleman's gentleman, but 'e's the only manservant in the 'ouse. 'Cept for old Methias, 'im as brings in the wood and tends the milch cows."

"Mr. Abbott?"

"The butler, sir."

"Ah, yes, Abbott. And your name?"

The girl curtsied again. "I be Trudy, my lord."

"And have you been at Holden House long, Trudy?"

"Since Friday last, my lord. Me pap took me to a hiring fair, and Mrs. Abbott give 'im ten shillings to let me come to 'Olden 'Ouse."

"Since Friday last," Ben repeated, though to himself. "Tell me, Trudy, have you been here long enough to meet *everyone* in the house?"

The girl's cheeks turned a fiery red, and she bent down to the hearth once again to finish laying the wood, her entire concentration centered upon the task. "B'aint nobody else in the 'ouse," she replied, her voice revealing a nervousness out of all proportion to the simple question Ben had asked. "Nobody at all, my lord. I swear there b'aint! 'Cept for the servants. Oh, and Miss Constance, of course."

"Of course." Ben hesitated only a moment, wishing he had not introduced the subject of the other inhabitant of the house. Since he had, however, he might as well follow through with it. "Tell me, Trudy, how is my great-aunt? Is she well?"

The girl exhaled loudly, as if relieved to discuss the elderly lady. "Yes, my lord. Miss Constance be well enough for one 'er age. 'Er stays in 'er rooms mostly. 'As 'er meals brought to 'er. But seems to me she be content enough, doing 'er stitching and all, and working on 'er bride clothes."

Ben winced. *Bride clothes.* Constance Holden, known in the family as "The Relic," was eighty years old if she was a day, yet she still looked for the return of the young lieutenant to whom she had given her heart nearly sixty years ago. James Whitcombe had gone off to the American colonies to fight in the French and Indian Wars, and he had never returned; or if he had come home, he had chosen to keep the fact a secret from his betrothed.

Constance was sister to the previous Lord Holden, as well as to Ben's grandfather, and like all the Holdens, she was, for lack of a better word, eccentric. According to Ben's old nanny—a woman who had known the three Holdens in their youth—Roland, Constance, and Geoffrey were all dicked in the nob.

Geoffrey, Ben's grandfather, was the youngest and arguably the sanest of the trio, but he had taken it into his head one day to see the Spice Islands, and off he had sailed, never to be heard from again. Not only did he abandon his brother and sister, but Geoffrey also left behind a son who spent weeks at a time locked in his bookroom translating treatises written by obscure fourth-century Greek philosophers; a daughter-in-law who made a life's work of quacking herself for imagi-

nary illnesses; and a young grandson who endured
years of bloody noses and black eyes, all earned while
fighting off the school bullies who thought it great
sport to taunt him with the history of his bizarre
family.

It was no wonder that when Ben grew to manhood,
he never spoke of his peculiar relatives. Let people believe whatever they wished of them and of him. He
had learned at an early age to admit nothing, to deny
nothing, and to justify nothing. In that way, he main-
tained his pride.

When notified that his great-uncle had died, and
that he had been declared the heir, Ben had been reluctant to take his place as head of a family with such
a reputation. He had not wanted to come north to
Holden House, even though there remained only him
and "The Relic," the last of the Holdens.

Ben had not seen his great-aunt since he was a boy
of perhaps ten or eleven, but he remembered her as a
harmless old lady, lost in her fantasy of a lover who
would return to her on the morrow. In her own vague
way, she had been kind to a lonely boy, and now that
Ben was the new Lord Holden, Great-aunt Constance
was his responsibility.

Last evening, when he had concocted his charade
about being an amnesiac, he had momentarily forgotten that "The Relic" was in residence. Now, it be-
hooved him to pay a visit upon his great-aunt before
Phoebe stumbled upon her. All too knowledgeable
about the idiosyncrasies of his family, he could not
even guess what his aunt might do if she came upon
Phoebe unawares. Or, for that matter, what Phoebe
might do if she encountered the elderly lady in some
dark corner.

Ben said no more to the maid, merely waited until
she had finished with the fire and quit the bedchamber, then he threw back the covers and hurried to the

dressing room. To his relief, his breeches and coat hung there, just as the maid had said. In too big a hurry to get to his great-aunt before Phoebe happened upon her, Ben did not worry over minor niceties such as shaving. There would be time for that later. For now, he must find Aunt Constance.

The shirt he had slept in was wrinkled beyond reclamation, so after removing it and tossing it on a chair, he had a quick wash, brushed his dark, thick hair back away from his face, then availed himself of one of his great-uncle's freshly starched shirts from the clothespress. As well, he chose one of Roland's least outdated cravats, and once the linen was tied neatly at his throat, Ben donned his coat, then strode quickly down the corridor and past the staircase.

The house, which his old nanny had proclaimed a curst rabbit warren—and a suitable abode for the harebrained trio who had been born there—was L-shaped, and the door that gave access to his great-aunt's part of the second floor was located just at the angle where the two corridors met.

Not that it looked like a door.

Nor did Ben bother knocking.

Instead, he reached inside a plaster wall niche, empty now of the bronze statue of Zeus that had fascinated the ten-year-old boy all those years ago, and pressed a button. Slowly, a narrow section of the wall slid opened.

Just as Ben remembered from his previous visit, the opening revealed a small landing perhaps five feet square, with a wrought-iron staircase—narrow and spiraled—that led to the ground floor. His aunt had used her own money to have the stairs installed the year after her soldier had not returned to wed her. She had insisted that as a spinster, she could not use the same staircase as her bachelor brother. Why that should be so, Ben had never discovered, but it was all

of a piece with the peculiar habits of the brother and
sister who had spent their eighty-plus years at
Holden House, growing battier by the decades.

On the other side of the landing, an actual door—
one possessing a latch and a key—stood open, and as
Ben drew near, he spied a portion of the sitting room
of his aunt's apartment. From what little he could see,
the room looked as though the old lady were holding
a jumble sale. Stacks of folded clothing lay on every
conceivable surface, with many of the stacks reaching
so high the topmost articles had fallen onto the lovely
old blue-and-gold carpet.

He heard his aunt's voice. Or he supposed it was
his aunt speaking. The voice was frailer than he remembered, with a quivery timbre that suggested the
elderly lady might be out of the habit of engaging in
long conversations.

He was about to announce his presence when he
saw her. Constance Holden had never been as tall or
as robust as her two brothers, who had both been
over six feet tall, but when Ben saw her twenty years
ago, she was of average height for a female. Now, she
seemed to have shrunk, both in size and in stature,
and even though her powdered wig gave her a few
added inches, Ben doubted she topped five feet.

Her wrinkled face was powdered, painted, and
patched, in the fashion prevalent in her youth, and
the hem of her green dress, which must have been
made for a much younger and much taller Constance,
dragged the floor with each step she took. How she
managed to move about without tripping on the ex-
cess of brocade, Ben could not say. In any event, she
did not have a free hand to lift the hem of her skirt,
the reason being that her arms were filled with what
appeared to be folded underthings, sewn from the
finest lawn.

"Here," she said to someone Ben could not see, "these should do nicely."

"Oh, no, ma'am. You are very kind, but I cannot accept."

Ben stifled a groan, for he recognized the voice. It belonged to Phoebe.

"And why can you not accept my gift?" Constance Holden asked, her tone decidedly miffed. "The items are new, and they are mine to give. I sewed them with my own hands."

"Yes, ma'am, and if I may say so, the needlework is exquisite, especially the delicately embroidered rose-buds on the night rail. But you told me those things were meant for your trousseau."

Trousseau! Ben swore beneath his breath. He should have guessed as much. Obviously, his great-aunt had already been prattling about her missing fiancé, the one she expected to return any day now, after a mere sixty years' absence!

Ben was glad he could not see Phoebe's face, though he could imagine how bewildered she must appear. Her normalcy had been one of the qualities that had drawn him to her eight years ago, and he would not be surprised if she was thanking her lucky stars this very moment that she had not married into such a family!

How the devil had those two met? Fast on the heels of that question came another: now that they had met, how the deuce was he to continue with his pretense of amnesia? Aunt Constance might have bats in her belfry, but the lawyer had assured Ben that she was not senile. If it was true, then she was certain to remember that her great-nephew had written her a letter of condolence last year when her brother, the previous Lord Holden, had died. And if she recalled the letter, Ben felt certain she would mention it the moment she saw him.

He was trying to think of some way to keep Phoebe from discovering his lie, and giving him the cut direct, when his aunt turned and spied him standing in the doorway. At first she only stared, her mouth agape, then she gasped and let fall the stack of petticoats, shifts, and drawers she held.

"Geoffrey," she said, the word little more than a whisper. Her lips began to tremble, and she raised her thin, quivering hand to her heart as if to keep that organ securely inside her chest. "Brother. Can it be you, come home at last?"

As Ben searched his mind for something to say—anything that would not give him away completely—his aunt seemed to rally, sudden anger giving her renewed strength. "Shame on you, Geoffrey Holden, for sailing away like that, and to some heathenish place I never even heard of. And not one word to Roland or to me since you left. Why, Mr. McNeese, the solicitor had you declared dead these past ten years and more!"

Chapter Six

While Ben stood in the doorway, not certain how to respond, Phoebe stepped forward and took Constance Holden's hands, holding the thin fingers carefully in her own. "Ma'am," she said gently, "I fear there has been a mistake. That gentleman is not your brother."

"Not Geoffrey?"

"No, ma'am. He is your great-nephew, the new Lord Holden."

"But he looks just like Geoffrey."

"Be that as it may, ma'am, he is not. That is *Bennett* Holden."

Phoebe turned toward Ben, and her eyes seemed to plead with him to let her do the talking—an entreaty Ben was more than happy to obey.

"Bennett?" Aunt Constance said. "Geoffrey's grandson?"

"Yes, ma'am. At least, I think he must be the grandson. He is most definitely the new heir."

Phoebe let go of one of the lady's hands and motioned for Ben to come closer. "My lord," she said, "here is your aunt, Miss Constance Holden." Her voice stressed the words, pointedly revealing the identity of the lady she believed Ben's amnesia would have caused him to forget.

His aunt gave Phoebe a searching look, one filled with such astuteness that Ben held his breath. "You speak as if the boy is dotty. Is he? Never tell me that his war wound left him too addlepated to remember his only remaining relative."

Recognizing his cue, and grateful for it, Ben came forward and made the old lady a very formal bow. "Aunt Constance," he said, "how wonderful to see you again. I hope I find you well."

From the smile on Phoebe's face, she was relieved to see that he had taken her hint and avoided any mention of amnesia. As for Ben, he could only thank the fates for helping him squeak by what could have been an end to his little scheme for revenge.

Aunt Constance allowed him to kiss her hand, the one on which she still wore the ring her fiancé had given her as a token of his affection. The ruby was too small to be of any real value, but obviously his aunt still prized it. As soon as Ben released her hand, she said, "Go away, there's a good boy, for you must know I never entertain gentlemen in my apartment. Besides, this young lady and I were just about to see what we could do to supply her with a few necessities until her trunks arrive."

She turned to Phoebe again. "I forgot, my dear. Why are you here?"

"The storm, ma'am. I spent the afternoon at Wen-lock Gorge, where the storm caught me, forcing me to seek shelter at Holden House. I live in the village of Coalport, and that is why I have no change of clothes with me."

"Oh, yes. I remember now. You may remain with us," Aunt Constance said, her tone as regal as that of an empress bestowing honors upon her subjects. "Only . . ."

"Only what?" Ben asked.

The elderly lady raised her hand to the side of her mouth, apparently under the misguided assumption that the bony fingers would act as a shield to keep

Ben from hearing the words she whispered to Phoebe. "You may not wish to remain," she said. "Because of my brother."

Perplexed, Ben could only stare, though Phoebe acted as though the remark were perfectly rational. "Which brother, ma'am?"

"Why, Roland, of course."

"Lord Holden? But, ma'am, his lordship passed away last year."

"I know that!" Constance said, her tone indignant. "Do you take me for an idiot?"

"Not at all, ma'am, it is just—"

"I attended his funeral," she continued, "even though I suffered from a debilitating catarrh for weeks afterward, due to the drafts that came through the warped doors of the old chaise. All the same, though Roland's body lies in the churchyard, I fear his spirit is not at peace. Lately, his ghost has begun to roam the corridors." She lowered her voice to a whisper once again. "He makes an unbelievable amount of noise."

Ghosts! Ben looked to see how Phoebe took this latest sign that his aunt's attic was to let. To his surprise, she merely smiled, then bent to retrieve the fallen linen.

"So that is the source of the noise I heard early this morning. You cannot know, ma'am, how relieved I am to hear that it is merely his lordship. I had feared it might be rats."

"Oh, no," Constance replied, "we do not have rats at Holden House. An occasional mouse, perhaps, but no rats. Though there were used to be some in the stables. Of course, I never visit the stables anymore."

Phoebe stood, the fallen linens draped over her arm. "A wise move, ma'am. Why should you bother with drafty old stables when you can remain in this very cozy apartment? Besides, all your things are

here, and you know where they are should you have
need of them."

Ben looked to see if Phoebe's countenance matched
her voice. Surprisingly, it did. She spoke softly, without the least hint of condescension, and when she
looked at his dotty old aunt—she with her powdered
wig and her painted face—the expression in Phoebe's
eyes was neither pitying nor judgmental.

Now, as he viewed those orbs in the full light of
day, Ben was obliged to admit that at least one of
Phoebe's features was even lovelier than he remembered. Her eyes were a smoky gray, like the sky before
a storm, and though they no longer bore the happy
twinkle he had once admired, there was about them
now a look of kindness, an unexpected gentleness, as
though their owner had grown more compassionate
with the years.

Last night, when Ben had observed Phoebe in the
candlelight, he had noticed that her face no longer
possessed the softness of youth. As he gazed at her
now, however, he decided there was something to be
said for sculpted cheekbones. She was handsomer
than he had thought upon first seeing her, and when
she smiled, as she was doing at the moment, she was
really rather pretty. If she were put in the hands of a
first-rate modiste, and had her hair cut and styled by
one of the current geniuses preferred by the fashionable ladies of the *ton*, Phoebe Lowell would pass for a
pretty woman any place.

Aware that Ben was staring at her, Phoebe pretended to concentrate upon folding the delicately
stitched linens and placing them on Constance
Holden's satinwood dressing table, the only piece of
furniture not already overflowing with bridal clothes.
With her back to Ben, Phoebe stole a glance at him in
the gold-rimmed demi-lune looking glass.

She had known the moment he began to watch her,

for she had felt his gaze upon her, and that knowledge had caused an unsettling flutter in her midsection. Now she took a moment to study him as well; the only difference was that from the slant of the small demi-lune, she could watch him without his knowing it.

She sighed, for Ben was probably comparing her to the beautiful London ladies who must vie for his attention now that he was a peer. Not that his title and wealth alone made him an eligible *parti*. Upon seeing him in the daylight, Phoebe could not believe how handsome he had become. Even more handsome than she had remembered.

Eight years ago, he had been only twenty-three, and a remaining bit of youth had gentled the features of his face. In the ensuing years, however, that gentling influence had disappeared completely, leaving in its place the hard angles and planes of a man fully grown—a man so heartbreakingly handsome, so dangerously masculine that Phoebe warned herself to be on her guard at every second, lest she lose her heart once again. And lose it she might, for at the moment she was having difficulty putting from her mind the remembered feel of that rugged face against her palm.

Last night, when she had checked his forehead to see if he had a fever, Ben had taken her hand and moved it down his face to his neck, and now as she watched him surveying her figure, an unreadable expression in his slightly hooded eyes, she wondered if he had known all along what he was doing. Had he been aware that the feel of his strong neck was playing havoc with her senses, sending a tingling sensation throughout her body?

During the wee hours of the morning, while Phoebe had sat by the fire, listening to Ben sleep, that tingling had haunted her, taunted her, daring her to stretch out her hand to touch him again. She had not done so,

of course, but the idea had warmed her face for hours.
Just as his slow scrutiny of her figure was warming
her at the moment.

He might or might not have been a rake eight years
ago, but from the way he was looking her over, she
doubted there was little the thirty-one-year-old Ben
did not know about the female form, amnesia or no
amnesia. What truly frightened Phoebe, however,
what caused her breath to catch in her throat, was her
total conviction that Ben Holden knew all too well
how to make a female forget her inhibitions . . . how
to make her yearn to be held once again against that
hard, unyielding chest.

Calling herself to saner, less dangerous thoughts,
Phoebe mentally checked off a list of all the reasons
why she was no longer an eligible candidate to be
Ben's wife—poverty and loss of social standing being
foremost. Not that he would ever ask her again.

A second list, even longer than the first, enumer-
ated the reasons why she could not let herself be the
object of his attentions for purposes *other* than marriage. A ruined reputation and a broken heart headed
that catalog, and by the time Phoebe had fixed the
final item firmly in her brain, her inhibitions were
safely in place.

Admonishing herself not to forgot them, she lowered her gaze from the looking glass and turned to
face the gentleman himself. "Well, sir," she said, "am I
to assume from the fact that you left your bed and are
dressed, that you are feeling more the thing this
morning?"

"He lacks manners," his aunt informed her, her
tone affronted, "for no true gentleman would call
upon a lady before he had shaved."

Phoebe had noticed the stubble herself. Unfortunately, the sight of it had caused a quite different reaction in her. Not the least affronted by his unshaven

face, she blushed to recall that she had wondered what such a cheek would feel like pressed against hers.

"Go, away!" the elderly lady ordered, her words recalling Phoebe to the present. "And do not let me see you again, sir, until you are presentable."

To Phoebe's relief, Ben did not take offense. "Your pardon, Aunt. I merely wished to pay my respects as soon as possible. Now that I have done so, I will do as you say, and take myself off. As it happens, I mean to take Miss Lowell off as well, so that she can choose which bedchamber she wishes to occupy for the remainder of her stay. She is to be our guest until the weather grows more forgiving of travelers, at which time she will return to the village and her place of employment."

"You are employed?" Aunt Constance asked.

"Yes, ma'am. At the china—"

"Do not tell me now, my dear, for I am fatigued, and I need to rest for a time."

"Yes, ma'am. Forgive me if I—"

"I have my tea at four of the clock," she said, already reaching for the woven basket containing her sewing items. "Come back then."

"What of me, Aunt? If I promise to shave, am I invited to drink tea with you as well?"

"Certainly not! Go away, there's a good lad, and do not bother me again. I am expecting someone, and if he should discover a male in my apartment, he might think I had not kept faith with my vow to wait for him."

Ben made no comment. He merely bowed to his aunt, motioned for Phoebe to precede him through to the landing, then closed the apartment door behind them. Not wanting to give himself away by revealing his knowledge of the secret entrance to his aunt's rooms, Ben escorted Phoebe down the wrought-iron staircase, going first to offer a barrier should she lose her step.

About midway down the spiral stairs, he stopped and turned to look at her. "How did you happen to meet my aunt?"

"She just appeared," Phoebe replied, "through a concealed door in the vestibule wall. As you can imagine, seeing her gave me quite a start."

"I can readily believe it would. It is not every day that an elderly woman materializes as if by magic. Especially not one dressed and coiffed like a figure from the previous century."

"Exactly." After a self-deprecating chuckle, Phoebe added, "You will think me the veriest goose, but during those first few moments, I thought she was a ghost."

"And once you discovered she was of this world, did it occur to you, given my aunt's strange appearance, that she might be deranged?"

"Deranged?" Phoebe shook her head. "Never. She is just a sweet old lady who clings to the past. Possibly because she was never given the future she had hoped for, poor dear."

"Poor dear? Then you find her an object for pity?"

Phoebe considered his question as though it were important. "Your aunt has my sympathy. After all, she had a dream that never came true, but I do not pity her. Over the past few years, I have met any number of people who have no dream at all—three of them bitter old ladies for whom I was a paid companion— and in my opinion, life without a dream of some sort is no life at all."

"And what," he asked quietly, "is your dream?"

As if surprised at the very personal question, Phoebe breathed in softly, and cocooned as they were in the quiet stairwell, Ben found the sound of that soft breath unbelievably intimate.

He stood one step below her, a circumstance that put their faces on a level, and with their mouths mere inches apart, Ben felt an almost overwhelming desire to taste Phoebe's lips. If she felt a similar desire, however, he was not to know, for she lowered her gaze and kept it lowered, as if to ensure her privacy. As for his question about her dream, she ignored that and continued with her answer about her feelings regarding his aunt.

"Though I am sorry Miss Holden's young man never returned to her, especially since marriage to him seems to have been her ambition in life, she is, nonetheless, one of the fortunate ones."

"Fortunate? How so?"

Phoebe looked at him once more. "Your aunt has let no one rob her of her hope that the dream might yet come true."

They said nothing more, merely continued to descend the stairs, coming out in the vestibule; after which, they climbed the broad, marble staircase to the next floor. Studiedly avoiding the wing to the right, which Ben knew held his aunt's apartment, he placed his hand at Phoebe's back and guided her to the left. "The master bedchamber you have already seen," he said, indicating the door at the far end of the corridor, "so unless you wish to spend a second night there, you had better choose from one of the four remaining rooms."

Phoebe ignored the warmth that rushed to her cheeks at the suggestion she might spend another night with Ben. Since he was being a perfect gentleman at present, there was no reason to suspect that he meant anything by that last remark, except to tease her. As if to prove her right, he reached around her to lift the latch of the first door, and as his face drew near hers, he winked.

"Sir," she said, relieved to see that he was, indeed,

trying to make her blush, "you always were an incorrigible tease."

"Was I?" he asked, his tone spuriously innocent. "My vocabulary is a bit rusty, so please enlighten me. Is incorrigible a synonym for delightful?"

Phoebe was hard pressed not to chuckle. "It is not, sir."

He sighed, as if disheartened. "I was afraid you would say it was not."

"If you would have a synonym for delightful, as it applies to you, allow me to tell you, on the chance that you have not already discovered it, that your dancing was always most *enjoyable*. Actually, it was you who taught me to waltz."

"Did I? Tell me more, Scheherazade. How was it I became your dancing instructor?"

"When you discovered that I had not yet learned that very fashionable dance, which was all the craze on the Continent, you would not be satisfied until I relented and allowed you to show me the steps. We spent all of one rainy afternoon at my uncle's town house, whirling around the drawing room, while my chaperone played waltz after waltz on the pianoforte. The poor thing wore her fingers to the bone, but you would not let her rest until I had the dance steps perfectly. Then, not content with browbeating poor Miss Barrington and me, you—"

"Browbeating? Surely that cannot be right."

"Would you have a synonym, sir? Very well. Not content with *bullying* Miss Barrington and me all afternoon, that evening at Almack's, you charmed one of the patronesses into giving her permission for me to stand up with you for my first waltz."

"How noble of me."

"Noble, indeed! Believe me, the other gentlemen did not share your view of the situation. Each time another man approached me, requesting my hand for the waltz, you scowled at him as though you might call him . . ." Phoebe let her voice trail off, for she had not meant to tell that part.

By the night of the waltz at Almack's, it had become obvious that Ben was very much in love with her. As for mentioning requests for her hand, that put her too much in mind of his marriage proposal, and she had no desire to remind him of that unfortunate incident.

Wanting to put some distance between them, she pushed against the door, whereupon Ben let go of the latch and stepped back, allowing her to enter the room. The walls in that bedchamber were papered with a subtle print of silver and lilac, with stripes of those colors in the pattern of the window drapery. It might once have been a pretty room. Unfortunately, at the moment the floor was covered in dust, and there was only one piece of furniture in evidence, an unimpressive oak washstand that had seen better days.

Adding to the forlorn atmosphere was the cold, dankness of the air inside and the sight of icicles hanging from the outside frames of the windows.

"Well," Ben said, "that is certainly odd. Shall we try another room?"

The other three rooms proved no more suitable than the first, with a small footstool in one; in another a dressing screen with an entire panel missing; and in the last room a small drop-leaf worktable. Since one of the legs was missing from the table, it lay rather dejectedly upon its side. Ben had said nothing after the first room, so Phoebe had no idea what was going on in his thoughts. Though if he was surprised by the state of this floor, he would really be shocked once he investigated belowstairs.

A muscle worked in the side of his jaw, and after a few moments, he crossed the dusty wooden floor in six long strides, then yanked on the bell pull. "Choose the bedchamber you prefer," he said, his jaw rigid, "and I will see that it is furnished within the hour. In the meantime, perhaps you would be more comfortable waiting in one of the ground-floor rooms."

Not wanting to be the one to tell him that his entire home was bare, Phoebe said, "I . . . uh, I prefer the silver and lilac."

She said no more, and once Ben heard her soft footfalls on the stairs, he gave the bell pull another series of yanks. Damnation! Had Roland Holden become a bedlamite in his later years? There could be no other excuse for all these empty rooms. What could his uncle have been thinking? And what the deuce had he done with the furniture?

According to Roland's solicitor, Mr. McNeese, who had visited Ben after his wound brought him back to England, the estate finances were in excellent shape, and the new Lord Holden figured as a very wealthy man. The attorney also warned Ben that scarcely a groat had been spent on the house in the past quarter century, preparing the new heir for a certain amount of shabbiness. But this . . . this was beyond anything!

Much of the furniture, and many of the art objects at Holden House had been collected by Ben's great-grandfather, reputedly a gentlemen of taste and discernment. And though Roland was the heir, for him to sell those items off was tantamount to thievery. It defied understanding how a man could be such a miser where expenditures were concerned, and yet sell off what amounted to a small fortune in family heirlooms.

Ben did not even want to consider what Phoebe must be thinking. She had called Aunt Constance a sweet old lady who clung to the past, but he doubted she would be as charitable in her estimation of the previous Lord Holden. The least she would call him was daft in the upper works, and even that assessment would be an understatement.

Furious with himself for not having looked over the house in private, before allowing anyone else to witness this embarrassing state of affairs, Ben was about to yank the bell pull again when he heard someone running up the rear stairs.

"Yes, my lord," said the young maid, her breath coming in gasps. "Can I be of 'elp, sir?"

"You can tell that poor excuse for a butler that I want to see him."

"Yes, sir," Trudy said, bobbing a nervous curtsy.

"And tell him that if he knows what is good for him, he will get himself up here on the double. And the housekeeper as well."

After bobbing another curtsy, Trudy turned and ran back the way she had come, hurrying as though the devil himself were after her.

Within little more than a minute, Ben heard heavier footfalls on the service stairs, then he spied the butler, followed closely by the housekeeper.

"Sir!" they said in unison, both red faced from their race up the stairs, and both of them assiduously keeping their eyes aimed toward their feet. The woman's lips trembled, and though she tried to hide her hands beneath the large apron she wore, it was obvious she was wringing them.

"I do not care how you do it," Ben began, his tone brooking no excuses, "but within the next half hour, I want the silver-and-lilac bedchamber clean enough to eat off the floor, and I expect to see it furnished in a manner adequate to the needs of my guest."

"Yes, my lord," they chorused.

"I will be belowstairs. As soon as the bedchamber is ready, with a fire going to take the chill from the air, you may send word. I will personally escort Miss Lowell to her quarters, to ensure that all is as I requested."

Ben did not ask even one question, and the moment

he had issued his final order, he turned and strode down the corridor toward the staircase, far too angry to look back.

"Phew," Henry Abbott said, still watching the retreating back of his new employer. "That were a close one, think on."

"Too close," his wife replied.

"I thought 'e'd called us up 'ere to say the jig were up."

"And what if he had? I warn you, Henry, I've no intention of spending the next twenty years of my life in Newgate prison."

"Never fear, my pet. It'll not come to that."

"So you say."

Abbott smiled, though the expression on his coarse face lacked real humor. "From the way 'is new lordship merely give us orders, never once asking for no explanation, I'd say 'e's probably as loony as the old lord."

"And what if you're wrong? This new one does not strike me as the least bit loony. It seemed to me he was far too angry to ask any questions. I stole a look into his eyes, and I tell you, Henry, I'd as soon not be around when he finds out what you've done."

"Not to worry, luv. The snow'll be gone soon, and once it's gone, so will we be, faster than the cat can lick 'er ear. Long before 'is lordship glims our lay."

"That's as may be, but what do you suggest we do in the meantime?"

"As to that, my pet, perhaps we should ask Mr. W."

"No, no! Do not say a word of this to him."

If the housekeeper had been nervous before, now she was positively pale with fear. "I don't trust that man, Henry, and if you had the brains Heaven gave a goat, neither would you."

"Aw, luv, 'e's all right, 'e is. A bit quick to anger, but 'e's got an 'ead on 'is shoulders."

"More fool you! That man is deranged, and he frightens me."

"You've no need to fret, my luv. When the time comes, I'll 'andle 'im."

"Handle him! You've addled your brain with ale. Mark my words, Henry Abbott, that one is a devil, and you'd be wise to step lightly around him. You cross him, and you'll wake one morning to find your throat slit from ear to ear."

Chapter Seven

Ben found Phoebe sitting on the bottom stair. Still angry, he spoke more harshly than he would have liked. "What the deuce are you doing here? Why did you not go into the drawing room?"

Vouchsafing no reply, she merely rose to her feet and walked to her left, toward what had once been his great-grandfather's undisputed sanctum. Always referred to as the gentlemen's withdrawing room, Ben remembered it well. Paneled in some sort of blackish wood from the Orient, it was decorated for a man's comfort, with large leather-covered brown chairs beside the fireplace, an oversize gaming table near the front windows, and a dark red carpet covering most of the floor.

Ben supposed he should not have been surprised to find the room empty. Somehow, though, seeing it not just bare, but also dirty and forlorn looking, caused an unexpected sadness inside him, almost as if his great-grandfather had been betrayed. Ben had never even known the man, yet he felt a strong desire to wring someone's neck on the old gentleman's behalf.

How dare Roland do this! How could a son hold so cheaply the things that had meant so much to his father? Did merely outliving another human being confer upon the survivor the right to discard all traces of the previous owner?

Ben had not been pleased to discover one very odd

proviso in his uncle's will, a stipulation that the heir must live a certain portion of each year at Holden House before he could gain control of the not inconsiderable amount of money left him by Roland Holden. In truth, Ben had not been all that happy about being the heir, for he wanted no part of the title or the house, for both brought back all the remembered humiliation that went with the name.

And yet, here in this room that was so much a part of his great-grandfather—the man his nanny had referred to as *Himself*—Ben felt a connection with all the Holdens who had come before him. The name and this house linked him with all those apparently normal generations who had preceded the very odd trio who were his grandfather, his great uncle, and his Aunt Constance.

"Once," he said, not realizing he spoke aloud, "Holden was a name to be proud of."

"And still is," Phoebe replied, her whispered words sounding overly loud in the cavernous space. "The entire village of Coalport can talk of nothing save the new Baron Holden. The villagers know little of you; only that you were decorated in the war, that you served in the Peninsular under Sir Arthur Wellesley, and that you retired a major from the Royal Regiment of Artillery. But believe me, sir, in the eyes of every man, woman, and child in the area, you are a hero, and they are proud that you are one of them."

Her statement startled Ben to such a degree that he could only stare, the emptiness of the room pushed to the back of his mind. "Are you having me on?"

"Am I what?"

"Making sport of me," he snapped. "Jesting at my expense."

It was Phoebe's turn to stare. "Why would I do such a thing?"

"Why, indeed?" he muttered. "Have the villagers

never spoken to you of the last baron and his sib-
lings?"

"Not really. From all I can gather, his lordship was a
bit of a recluse, even before his protracted illness, and
he never left the estate. For that reason, most of the
people I know had never even seen him. As for Miss
Constance, until I met her an hour ago, I had no idea
of her existence. The only Holden the villagers discuss
is you. And even though they do not know you, they
take a certain pride in your accomplishments. They
cannot wait for you to take up residence."

Ben was speechless.

"I am sorry," she said.

"For what?"

"That you find your house in such disrepair. In this
instance, perhaps your amnesia is a blessing. After all,
if you cannot remember the house as it was, you cannot mourn the loss of familiar objects."

For the moment, Ben had forgotten his supposed
amnesia. How ironic that when his mind was being
flooded with memories, he must be on his guard to
pretend that he recalled nothing.

"I fear," Phoebe continued, "that you will find the
room across the vestibule no more inviting than this
one. It, too, is empty. When I was in there last, I noticed what appeared to be an archway in the far wall,
so I assume there must be other rooms farther along."

Yes, Ben had run through that archway as a lad, to
the light, airy morning room painted in shades of pale
yellow and decorated with delicate white-and-gilt
French chairs. He had liked the sunny yellow, as well
as the warm red of the companion room next to it,
with its wing-tipped harpsichord fashioned of inlaid
satinwood. Beyond that was the library, another room
that was sacrosanct, and off limits to a small boy.

"I did not investigate," Phoebe said, "but perhaps
you will find those other rooms a pleasant surprise."

"Somehow, I doubt it."

Though he had not meant to do so, Ben caught her hand and began pulling her along behind him, toward the vestibule. "Come," he said. "If I must wander through a maze of abandoned rooms, I shall need a bit of company. Too bad we have not a cache of bread crumbs so we might leave a trail to follow, should we get lost."

"That is what you said the last time."

Ben paused and looked back at her. "Excuse me?"

"You and I were in a maze once, the famous one on the grounds at Edgarton Hall, and you made that same remark about the bread crumbs."

Here was something Ben truly had forgotten. "We were lost in a maze?"

She lifted her chin in spurious indignation. "Only one of us was lost, my lord. As it turned out, *you* had a map to the maze in your pocket the entire time. You had purchased it when you paid the gardener to let us take a turn in the gardens. Though, for devious reasons of your own, you had neglected to apprise me, or my chaperone, of the map."

Ben laughed. Now he recalled the incident. While in that maze, he had finally gotten up the nerve to kiss Phoebe. That was all he had remembered of the day, the taste of her sweet lips. "Am I correct in assuming we gave your dragon the slip?"

"Miss Barrington? Oh, yes. Poor soul."

Though Phoebe tried to keep a straight face, a chuckle escaped her. It had been a wonderful afternoon, and she and Ben had run ahead of her chaperone, two young people escaping for a moment of privacy. They had left Miss Barrington behind, and from the other side of the shrubbery they could hear the middle-aged lady moving about, trying to find the way out, yet discovering only solid walls of greenery.

"You held my hand then," Phoebe reminded him,

"just as you are doing now, all but pulling me along in your hurry to escape Miss B."

"And what was the result of that escape? Did we find a secluded corner and a few moments of privacy?"

Ben watched the color creep into her face, and he knew the instant she recalled the kiss. "You need not answer," he said, "for your face gives you away." He lifted his hand and touched her temple, smoothing his fingertips slowly down to her jaw, enjoying the satiny feel of her skin. "Did I steal a kiss?" he whispered.

Phoebe did not think she had ever experienced anything as wonderful as the feel of Ben's fingertips sliding across her skin. When he asked her about the kiss, she held her breath, unmoving, all but willing him to steal another. In the silence that followed, he searched her eyes, as if judging her receptivity, then he leaned toward her until he was so close she could feel the warmth of his breath against her lips.

"Shall I steal another?" he whispered.

Yes! Yes!

While Phoebe's heart begged her to answer in the affirmative, her brain spoiled sport by reminding her of that mental list she had gone over not an hour ago—that list of reasons why she must not allow herself to be the object of any romantic overtures from Ben. "You did not steal a kiss," she said, "for you were too much the gentleman to take advantage of the situation."

"Liar," he said, then he laughed to take the sting from the word.

Ignoring the seductiveness of his throaty laugh, Phoebe stepped back out of temptation's way and slipped her hand from his. "Bread crumbs or not," she said, "perhaps we had better have a look at the remainder of this floor. That is, if you still want my company."

He made her an abbreviated bow. "After you, Miss Lowell." The playfulness was gone from his voice, and this time he did not offer to take her hand. "The sad fact is," he said, "that should we lose our way, we need only follow the footprints we leave in the dust."

Within a matter of minutes, they had crossed the empty drawing room and passed through the archway. Ben did not linger in those denuded twin chambers, but continued through the pocket doors that gave access to the library. One entire wall contained floor-to-ceiling bookshelves, but any books that may have once resided there were no longer in evidence.

Aside from the missing printed matter, however, the room was a pleasant surprise. At one end it boasted a handsome walnut knee-hole desk and a leather-bottom chair, both of which were at least a century old. While at the opposite end, on either side of the large fireplace, with its carved oak mantel and surround, stood a settee upholstered in faded gold brocade, and a wing chair in tan leather. Of the brass andirons and wood box there was not a sign. Gone, too, were the crystal lamps and the silver candlesticks, though a worn but still serviceable turkey carpet remained, covering the hardwood floor.

After looking around him, Ben expelled a long breath, almost as if he had been holding it the entire time.

Phoebe exhaled as well, with relief. "What a handsome room," she said.

"And how gratifying," Ben added, "to finally discover a bit of furniture. I had begun to wonder if we were destined to search forever for a place to sit."

After taking a second, slower look, Ben stared at the wooden ladder that slid from one end of the book cases to the other, giving access to the upper shelves. The ladder possessed a folding seat, and between the seat and the lower rungs someone had stuffed a rather peculiar-looking object. Oblong and shaggy, from a distance the thing resembled nothing so much as an English sheepdog, head and all.

"Famous!" Ben said. "I cannot believe it!"

While Phoebe remained at a prudent distance, she watched Ben make short work of the space between the fireplace and the ladder. As he drew close to the furry object, he began to chuckle, though what he found amusing, she could not even guess. Of one thing only was she certain: whatever the object was, it was no English sheepdog. Not with those long, yellowed teeth. "What is it?"

Ben did not reply. Instead, he laid the large, cumbersome item on the floor. Then using the toe of his boot, he pushed it, unrolling it until it lay flat. Or as flat as was possible, considering the presence of the massive white head.

"I ask again, my lord. What is it?"

"It is a polar bear. Or it was once. Since the underside has been fitted with a jute lining, one can only assume that it is meant to be a rug."

Phoebe shuddered. "A rug with teeth. How charming."

"Come closer," he said, "have a look. It will not bite you."

"And I am to take your word for that?"

"Of course. Would I mislead you?"

"The old Ben might."

"Come, I will show you." When she did not move, Ben bent down and placed his open hand between the fearsome-looking fangs. "See," he said, "nothing to worry ab— Ohhhh!"

With a moan, he fell to his knees, his hand still between the creature's teeth, and Phoebe screamed.

Terrified, she raced across the room. Reaching over Ben's shoulders, she grabbed for his arm, pulling with all her strength. The arm came away surprisingly easily, and when he waved his fingers in front of her face, all five of them whole and unbloodied, Phoebe saw red of another kind.

"Ben Holden!" she yelled, fear and fury combining to rob her of needed breath, "you are . . . are . . . despicable!" Unable to restrain herself, she put her hands around his throat and squeezed.

He let her have her revenge for a moment before he reached up and caught her wrists, pulling her down beside him on the furry rug. He was laughing, and in time Phoebe could not resist the lure of his smiling eyes. "You have not changed a bit."

Still laughing, he said, "The jest worked better than I could have expected. Will you forgive me?"

"Never!" She yanked her wrists from his grasp. "You frightened the very wits out of me. I thought you were injured."

When she grew still, he spoke quietly, his voice contrite. "You are right, I am despicable."

"Very."

"And you," he said softly, "are very tender hearted." Ben captured her face between his hands and looked deeply into her eyes. "I am sorry," he said.

When she did not reply, he stroked his thumbs across the sensitive skin beneath her cheekbones, his touch so gentle Phoebe forgot all else save the mesmerizing touch of his hands and the fact that their bodies were so close she had felt the rumble of his chest when he laughed. She felt something else as well, the masculine strength of his hard body, and the almost frightening longing inside her to have him take her in his arms.

"Phoebe," he whispered.

The sound of her name upon his lips caused a fluttering inside her chest, like the wings of some long imprisoned bird sensing freedom at last. Like that bird, Phoebe was terrified of what would come next, yet her heart would not let her pull away.

Still holding her face between his hands, Ben bent his head and brushed his lips against hers, the touch so soft she would not have believed he had actually kissed her if it were not for the warmth that spread all the way to her toes. She waited, not daring to breathe, while he bent his head a second time. Their lips had only just touched when there was a sound from the doorway.

"Your pardon, my lord," a young maid said, her head bowed and her attention concentrated upon the hem of the apron she twisted in her hands.

"Yes," Ben said, his voice edged with irritation, "what is it, Trudy?"

"Mrs. Abbott sent me, my lord. The lady's bedchamber be ready."

At four that afternoon, Ben chose to ignore Constance Holden's command not to return to her apartment. He made his appearance just after the maid arrived with the tea tray, and though his great-aunt frowned at him in a most disapproving manner, he smiled pleasantly at her.

"Take yourself away," Aunt Constance said.

"Good afternoon, Aunt. May I?" he asked, indicating a lyre-back chair. Without waiting for permission, he removed a stack of never-worn, filmy night dresses from the upholstered seat and set them on the floor. After which, he brought the chair over to the small gait-leg table that held the tea things, then joined his aunt and Phoebe. "Umm," he said, inhaling deeply of the aromatic steam coming from the cobalt blue teapot, "something smells wonderful."

As it turned out, he exerted himself during the next hour to entertain his relative, causing her to laugh aloud after a highly dramatized account of their guest's aversion to polar bears. So amused was the elderly lady that she forgot all about her decree against male company.

"What foolishness," she said, using a finely sewn wisp of linen to dab at the tears of laughter that coursed down her rouged cheeks. "And I warn you, sir, I do not believe a word of it."

Ben placed his hand over his heart, as if wounded by her lack of trust in his word. "I vow, Aunt Constance, I speak only the truth."

After a wink in Phoebe's direction, to thank her for allowing him to tell the story to her disadvantage, he held his empty cup out for her to refill. "In all honesty, it never occurred to me that a seemingly sensible female like Miss Lowell would be afraid of a rug. Even one with teeth."

"Big, *yellow* teeth," Phoebe corrected him, giving him a look that said he would pay for this later.

Lifting the teapot, she filled Ben's cup with the steaming, mahogany-colored brew, then turned to their hostess. "Ma'am?" she said. "May I freshen your tea?"

"No, thank you, my dear. One cup is sufficient for my needs. But you go ahead, do, and while you are about it, finish up that last salmon tartlet. And pass Ben the macaroons. The lad was always fond of sweet treats."

"I enjoy them still," he said. While he spoke, his gaze settled on Phoebe's lips, his eyes sparkling with devilment. "Especially when they are soft and pliant."

Phoebe's breath caught in her throat, for she was certain the sweet treats he referred to were not the sort produced in the kitchen.

Though their kiss had been interrupted, Phoebe fancied she could feel it still. If she closed her eyes, she could imagine that Ben's strong hands were framing her face, holding her gently, as one might hold a captured bird, while his firm lips claimed hers, seducing her into a response.

And she had definitely responded!

Of course, she should not have let him kiss her. It was a mistake, a result of the fright she had sustained due to his jest about the bear biting his hand. Her fear, combined with the closeness of their bodies, made the moment emotionally charged, and Phoebe had all but fallen into his arms. But she would see that nothing like that happened again.

She thanked the powers that be for sending Trudy to interrupt their embrace. No matter what, Phoebe could not let Ben kiss her again. She *would* not let him kiss her again.

"So," Ben said, bringing her thoughts back to the moment, "I believe you mentioned earlier, madam, that you were once a paid companion."

"Actually," she replied, popping the last morsel of salmon tartlet into her mouth, then licking bits of the flaky crust from her fingertips, "I was a companion more than once. Three times, to be exact, and they were all very *short* times. Needless to say, I was not a success at the position."

"Why was that?" Miss Constance asked. "You are such an amiable young lady, my dear, that I cannot imagine the fault was yours."

"Oh, I assure you, ma'am, the fault was almost entirely mine. You are kind to call me amiable, but in truth, I have rather an unyielding personality. Though I promised myself with each new employer that I would guard my tongue and curb my rebellious nature, the sad truth is that I kept forgetting my vow."

She sighed, as if loath to admit her additional shortcomings. "I am not overfond of criticism—no matter how constructive—and that failing, in conjunction with my total lack of humility, resulted in my being turned off all three times. The last time, without a reference."

Surprised, Ben said, "Surely you are in jest. How is

a female to secure a new position without a reference from her previous employer?"

"Unfortunately, that particular previous employer did not concern herself with my welfare. She was a thoughtless, ill-tempered old lady, and after she threw a book at me for daring to suggest that she would retain her servants longer if she did not yell at them, I told her exactly what I thought of her manners, her intelligence, and her breeding. Or more to the point, her lack of breeding."

"Good for you!" Ben said.

"Not at all, my lord, for I was turned out that very day. Since I had been part of the household for less than a week, my employer refused to pay me what was owed, and I was obliged to spend my last five pounds on the coach ride back to London. After that, I was forced to admit that mine is an obstinate nature. Which, I assure you, is not an attribute to be desired in a female seeking employment in a genteel establishment."

The story was related as if it were a good joke on Phoebe, and Ben found himself admiring her strength. In a matter-of-fact manner, without the least hint of self-pity, she had condensed what must have been a very difficult few years in her life.

"Is your home in London, my dear?"

"No, ma'am. I reside in Coalport, not far from the pottery factory where I am employed."

"But what of your real home? Your family?"

Phoebe hesitated, and Ben could see that she was uncomfortable with this very personal line of questioning. To turn his aunt's thoughts, he asked her if she had been able to prevail upon Phoebe to accept a few items of clothing. "From this overflowing cache," he said, looking around him at the result of more than half a century's needlework.

As if grateful to him for changing the subject, Phoebe said, "Miss Constance has been very generous, my lord. Earlier this afternoon, she sent Trudy to my bedchamber with a more than ample supply of beautiful linens and *fol lols*."

"*Fol lols*?" he asked. "Surely you cannot mean such fripperies as fans and reticules?"

"Something better," she replied, lifting the hem of her skirt a half inch above her boot top to reveal a white lisle stocking, clocked in pale blue. "And I cannot tell you, sir, what a pleasure it is to wear warm, dry hosiery."

"Actually," Ben said, pretending to raise a quizzing glass to his eye, the better to leer at her ankle, "the pleasure is entirely mine."

"Sir," his great-aunt said, "behave yourself."

"Yes, ma'am. I shall sit here quiet as a mouse, without uttering another word. All in the hope that our guest has some other, perhaps even more interesting *fol lol* in mind to show us."

"Oh, I have," Phoebe replied.

"Truly?" he asked, not a little surprised at her uninhibited reply.

With her lips twitching at the corners, as though she tried to stop a smile from becoming full-blown, she reached inside the sleeve of her dress and removed a lace-edged handkerchief. "Is this the sort of thing you had in mind, Lord Holden?"

He chuckled. "No, Miss Lowell, it is not. And well you know it."

"La, sir, I cannot think what you mean."

"He means to make a pest of himself," his aunt interjected, waving her hands at Ben as if to shoo him away. "I wish you will leave us," she said, "and next time wait for an invitation before insinuating yourself where you are not wanted. Now, be off with you, for I have work to do before I retire for the night."

"As you wish," Ben said. Not the least insulted, he kissed his aunt's proffered hand and wished her sweet dreams. Phoebe rose as well, thanked her hostess for the lovely tea, and bid her a good evening. Moments later, the two guests were once again descending the spiral staircase.

"Will you join me in the library?" Ben asked. "We can have supper served in there later."

"I think not," Phoebe replied, still much too conscious of what had happened between them the last time they were alone in that room. "If you will excuse me, my lord, it has been a very long day, and I should like to follow your aunt's example and retire early."

The look Ben gave her said he did not believe her excuse. "Come now, madam, never tell me you are turning missish on me. After all, we spent most of last night together in the same bedchamber, *sans* chaperon." He lowered his voice to a whisper. "What is going on in that pretty head of yours? Are you afraid to be alone with me?"

Yes! Frightened clear out of my mind!

"Was it the kiss?" he asked.

When she did not reply, he caught her hand and turned it over, exposing the tender flesh of the inside of her wrist. Slowly, deliberately, he moistened his lips, then pressed them against that sensitive flesh, holding them there while he spoke again, his voice so low, so soft, it had a sleepy quality. "Is it me you are afraid of, my sweet? Or could it be yourself?"

Not wanting to tell him what his whispered words did to the rhythm of her breathing, or what the feel of his lips upon her skin did to her resolve not to become his current flirt, Phoebe pretended to laugh. "Afraid of you, my lord? Never.

"However," she added, trying for a careless tone, "I shall keep to myself my continued misgivings about the polar bear."

Chapter Eight

The sound of Ben's laughter followed Phoebe up the broad staircase. She rather enjoyed his laugh, but her legs almost failed her, knowing that he stood just as she had left him, watching her climb the stairs, watching the sway of her hips, and probably imagining what she looked like without her skirt obscuring his view of the borrowed lawn underpinnings.

Unwilling to let him know that she was aware of his scrutiny, she did not glance behind her once she reached the top stair. Instead, she turned left and continued down the corridor to the bedchamber that had been prepared for her.

"The lady's bedchamber be ready," the maid had said earlier that afternoon, while she stood in doorway of the library.

The young servant had turned several shades of red, apparently mortified to have discovered her new master and his guest on their knees on a bearskin rug, kissing. At the sound of the servant's voice, Ben had jumped to his feet, held his hand down to assist Phoebe to rise, then together they had followed the scarlet-faced Trudy to the vestibule and up the marble staircase to the silver-and-lilac bedchamber.

To Phoebe's surprise, the appearance of the room was far different from what it had been an hour earlier. The bare floor was clean, and smelled pleasantly of rose-scented bee's wax, and though there were few furnishings, the room was imminently inviting.

The unimpressive oak washstand that had been there earlier had been wiped clean and set in the far corner, with an earthenware bowl and pitcher on the top. A narrow cot, perhaps brought down from the servants' rooms in the attic, had been made up with fresh sheets, then covered with a pretty pink counterpane and two fluffy pillows. To the right of the bed stood a small table, complete with a pewter candlestick and an oxide bottle, and on a wall peg in the far corner someone had hung Phoebe's blue cloak.

A fire had been lit in the fireplace, and the air was warm and inviting. From the look on Ben's face, he was far from happy with the results, but Phoebe could not have been more pleased. Her accommodations in Coalport were nowhere near this comfortable, and at Mrs. Curdy's she did not have the luxury of a fire or this blessed privacy.

Now, as Phoebe opened the door of the bedchamber, she looked forward to that privacy. The fire had all but burned itself out, but the room was still cozy compared to the chill of the corridor. Someone—Trudy, she imagined—had brought her a tin of hot water, a small bar of scented soap, and a brush, and after turning the key in the lock, Phoebe stripped completely bare and washed herself all over before slipping into one of the nightdresses lent her by Miss Constance.

Enjoying the feel of being genuinely clean for the first time since she left Mrs. Curdy's yesterday, Phoebe brushed out her long, thick hair, letting it hang free about her back and shoulders; then, she crossed to the cot and crawled beneath the covers. It was not quite dark outside, and while she lay in her narrow bed, gazing out through the partially frosted windowpanes, her thoughts returned to that much larger bed down the corridor, the bed she had inadvertently shared with Ben.

Perhaps it was recalling the sensation of being held close in Ben's arms the night before, his naked body pressed against hers, or perhaps it was merely the sensual pleasure of the fine lawn of the nightdress brushing her skin, in any event, the moment she fell asleep she began to dream. In the dreams, she and someone tall and strong—Ben, she supposed—waltzed in a brightly lit ballroom, their bodies in perfect harmony, while beautiful music played all around them.

Later, the dark-haired man of her dream led her into a glass conservatory filled to the very ceiling with sweet, fragrant flowers, and there he took her in his arms again. Only this time, he kissed her, and as his lips trailed fiery kisses from her neck to her ear and back to her mouth, awakening every inch of her body, he whispered, "Will you be mine, lovely Phoebe?"

Her heart bursting with joy, she said, "Yes, my love, I will be yours. Forever."

"Forever?" he said, his voice so silky she almost lost the meaning of his words. "What do we need with forever? It is but a word."

"Yes, but—"

"Sweet girl, I wish you to be mine, but only for tonight."

Phoebe came awake with a gasp, her heart pounding so hard against her chest she thought it meant to escape. As she sat there in the darkness, shivering from the coldness of the room, she realized the fire had finally burned itself out, leaving her in a strange place with neither warmth nor light. Recalling the pewter candlestick on the bedside table, she felt around for the oxide bottle, lit the spill, then used it to light the candle.

Once the soft illumination had rid the room of its

strangeness, Phoebe slipped her feet into the serviceable woolen bed slippers Miss Constance had given
her and crossed to the hearth to put another log on
the andirons. Soon she had a fire going, and the
warmth of the orange and blue flames dispelled the
last of the unsettling dream. With the disappearance
of the dream, normality returned, and Phoebe realized her foolishness in going to bed without supper.
Her stomach felt as though she had not eaten in days,
and her throat was parched for something soothing to
drink.

Thinking she might find a bit of cheese in the
larder, and perhaps some milk she could warm to
take back up to her room with her, she fetched her
cloak from the peg and draped the woolen folds over
her shoulders, not bothering to fasten the frog at her
neck. With the hems of her cloak and her nightdress
in one hand and the candle in the other, she exited the
bedchamber and went belowstairs.

The house slippers made only a whisper of sound
on the marble stairs and the short corridor that led to
the kitchen, and remembering the bumping noises in
the walls—noises she had attributed to rats—Phoebe
breathed a sigh of relief when she reached the kitchen
without encountering any unpleasant creature. To her
dismay, that sigh proved precipitous, for the instant
she opened the kitchen door, she bumped into a creature able to do her far more harm than a mere rodent.

Having collided with a solid wall of living, breathing manhood, Phoebe screamed.

"Be quiet," the man said, placing his right hand
across her mouth and grabbing her round the waist
with his left arm. "I should hate to be obliged to use
force to silence you."

In her fright, Phoebe had dropped her candle, so
she used both hands to push against the man's chest,
trying in vain to free herself. The man merely laughed,

and while she struggled, he yanked her tightly against his slender body. He smelled faintly of brandy and damp wool, and his coat was liberally sprinkled with snowflakes. "If you promise to be quiet," he said very close to her ear, "I will remove my hand from your mouth and reward you with a kiss."

Appalled at the suggestion, Phoebe tried again to push free of his embrace. Her bid for freedom did not prove successful, and in desperation, she stomped his foot. Unfortunately, due to her cloth slippers and his heavy boots, she did more damage to her own foot than to his. The man laughed at her fruitless attempts, a circumstance that angered Phoebe more than she could say; then, before she knew what was happening, he moved the hand that held her silent and quickly replaced it with his mouth.

Catching her by the hair, he forced her head back, kissing her in a brutish manner that ground her lips against her teeth, all the while holding her body so close she nearly fainted from lack of air. Sickened by his kiss, yet unable to stop his cruel onslaught, Phoebe employed a maneuver one of the other china painters had told her worked every time on men who would not take no for an answer. Hoping the girl was correct, Phoebe lifted her knee, and brought it straight up with all the force she could muster.

The move worked even better than she had hoped, for the instant her knee made contact, the man released her. With a cry of pain, he fell back against the deal table, knocking it and the bench aside. He could not break his fall, because both his hands were engaged in holding that very private area between his legs.

Feeling not even an ounce of remorse for having inflicted such unexpected pain upon a fellow human being, Phoebe turned and fled down the short corridor. Her cloak fell away from her shoulders, but she did not stop to retrieve it. She was far too busy making her way up the broad staircase, her one wish to attain her bedchamber and turn the key in the lock.

Without the aid of her candle, the area at the top of the stairs was engulfed in sheer darkness, and as she reached it, she ran into another solid wall of maleness. This time, however, Phoebe recognized both the voice that urged her to silence and the muscular arms that went around her in a protective manner. Feeling as though she had found her heart's haven, she slipped her arms around Ben's robed waist and clung to him as though she meant never to let him go.

"What is amiss?" he said, his breath stirring a loose curl at her temple. "I heard a scream."

"A man," she said, her breathing labored, "in the kitchen. He . . . he would not . . ."

"Would not what?" Ben asked, taking her by the shoulders and putting her away from him where he could look into her face. "Tell me, Phoebe."

"He would not let me go. He . . . kissed me hard . . . so hard my lips ached . . . and—"

"Damn his eyes! I'll kill the bastard!" Ben took a deep breath, as if to control his anger, and when he spoke again, it was in a softer voice. "Did he hurt you?"

Phoebe was no longer a naive young girl. She knew what sort of hurt he referred to, and it had nothing to do with her bruised mouth. "No. He merely kissed me. But I . . . I hurt him."

"You did? Good for you."

Without another word, Ben put his arm around her shoulders and led her to her bedchamber. "Close the door," he ordered, his tone brooking no argument, "and lock it. Do not open it until I return."

More than willing to do as he asked, Phoebe turned the key in the lock, then hurried over to the warmth of the fireplace, trembling now that the danger had passed.

Ben trembled as well, but with rage. As he tiptoed down the stairs, quiet as a stalking tiger, his fingers closed around the pistol tucked into his waistband, ready and oh-so willing to do damage to whoever had tried to force himself upon Phoebe.

In the darkness, he nearly tripped on Phoebe's cloak, and though he managed not to give vent to his anger by cursing, the incident slowed his progress. When he finally reached the kitchen, he found it empty, save for those furnishings one might expect in such a room.

Taking a spill from the wide oak mantelpiece and lighting it in the banked embers of the cookfire, Ben looked all around the room. There was no sign of a man, though the table and the bench beneath it were pushed aside, as though someone had fallen against them.

He did find one thing, wet boot prints near the door that led to the kitchen garden. Someone had been there right enough, and within the last few minutes. Not that Ben had doubted Phoebe's story. If she said a man had accosted her, then it was true.

What was going on in this house? Whatever it was, Ben could no longer pass it off as the actions of his peculiar relatives. His great-aunt was too old to be up to mischief, the previous lord was dead and buried, and Ben had no other relatives—dotty or otherwise—who would feel themselves entitled to run free in his home. As for Aunt Constance's belief that the house was being haunted by her brother's ghost, that idea was so preposterous it was laughable—or it would be laughable if Phoebe had not been attacked.

Whoever she had surprised had been all too real, and first thing tomorrow Ben meant to discover the intruder's identity and what he was doing here. Unfortunately, all that would have to wait; at the moment a young woman was upstairs, alone and frightened.

Unable to find anyone upon whom to vent his anger, Ben returned to the corridor, retrieved Phoebe's cloak, and took the stairs two at a time. Within a matter of seconds, he tapped at her bedchamber door. "It is I," he said.

He heard her dash across the room, then turn the key, and when she opened the door, she flew into his arms once again. Without a word, he draped the cloak around her shivering body, then scooped her into his arms and carried her down to the master bedchamber. After kicking the door shut behind him, he crossed to the fireplace and the Windsor chair, where he seated himself, with Phoebe still in his arms.

Neither of them spoke for a time. Ben just held her close, his arms around her slender form, and her head resting upon his chest. Her hair hung loose, tumbling down her back like a bolt of pale brown silk, and occasionally Ben gave himself the pleasure of stroking the soft strands.

As for Phoebe, though she soon ceased to tremble, her fear long gone, she made no effort whatever to apprise Ben of the fact. Had she done so, she might have been obliged to leave the comfort of his embrace, and that was the last thing in the world she wished to do. She had never known such contentment. She could not remember ever before being carried in a man's arms—not even her father's—and as for sitting on a gentleman's lap, that thought had never even occurred to her.

After a time, with Ben holding her close and allowing her to snuggle against his chest, Phoebe decided that the fright she had endured in the kitchen might have been worth it. In fact, she would do it again, if she could be certain Ben would rescue her and hold her like this.

Being in his arms might not be Heaven, but it was indisputably the next best thing.

"Care to tell me," he said after a time, "exactly what happened? Why were you belowstairs?"

"I was hungry. As ill luck would have it, I had just reached the kitchen when I bumped into that man. Literally."

"Did you recognize him? Might it have been Abbott?"

Phoebe shook her head. "There was very little light, so I did not see his face, but I can assure you, the man I encountered was not the butler. This fellow, though frighteningly strong, was quite slender. He was as tall as you, though perhaps a full two stone lighter, and not nearly so . . . so muscular."

To her surprise, Ben rewarded this last remark with a squeeze that brought her face very close to the open neck of his nightshirt, a circumstance that tempted Phoebe to touch her lips to that portion of his hard, exposed chest. Fortunately, she mastered the temptation before subjecting Ben, or herself, to embarrassment.

"He smelled of brandy," she said, continuing her description of the man in the kitchen, "and he wore a dark driving coat and light-colored breeches."

Phoebe's face grew uncomfortably warm, picturing the man while he held that injured portion of his anatomy, and she hoped Ben would not ask her how she happened to notice the color of his breeches. "His coat was damp with melting snow," she hurried to add, "as though he had just come in from outdoors, and I believe he was as surprised to see me as I was to see him."

After searching her memory for any further pertinent information, she said, "Oh, and now I think of it, his speech was more refined than the butler's, though not quite the voice of a gentleman. Still, I feel certain the man was educated."

For a time, Phoebe and Ben were both silent, the only sound coming from the fireplace where a bit of heated resin popped softly. "Do you think you could sleep now?" he asked.

Though unhappy with any suggestion that would oblige her to leave the delicious warmth of Ben's arms, Phoebe kept her real wish to herself. Suppressing a sigh, she said, "I suppose it is time I returned to my room."

"You will remain here," he said, the decisiveness in his voice informing her that the subject was not a matter for discussion. "In my bed."

Phoebe held her breath, not daring to ask him where he meant to sleep.

As if reading her thoughts, he said, "You sat up with me last night. Tonight it will my pleasure to do the same for you."

With that, he stood, allowing her cloak to fall to the floor, then carried her over to the enormous tester bed, with its thick, elaborately carved ebony posts. After laying her down very carefully on the side of the bed closest to the fire—the side on which he had slept the night before—he stood looking down at her, his gaze sliding over the full length of her, covered in only the thin lawn nightdress.

Something unreadable showed in his dark eyes, but before Phoebe could determine what it was, he pulled the covers up over her shoulders, tucking the ends beneath her chin.

"Ben, I—"

"Shh," he said.

Reaching out his hand, he placed the tips of his thumb and forefinger very gently on her eyelids, encouraging them to close. "Sleep," he whispered. "I will see that nothing disturbs your rest."

And what, she wondered, if the disturbance was Ben himself? Phoebe fell asleep wondering what she would have done if Ben had bent down at that moment and kissed her.

Ben asked himself much the same question. Except that his query went much further than a possible kiss. While he returned to the Windsor chair beside the fire, the thought uppermost in his mind concerned a list of ways he might have divested Phoebe of her filmy nightdress.

Had she but known it, that deceptively virginal article of clothing, with its long sleeves and its snugly tied collar, had revealed far more of her delectable figure than it had concealed. And what Ben saw was more than enough to heat his blood and send it racing to every part of his body.

Before he had pulled the covers up, he had looked his fill of her, unashamedly enjoying the sight of Phoebe with her lovely hair spread out about her on the pillow, and the folds of the near-transparent lawn hugging her rounded hips and her slender waist. At that moment, it had been all Ben could do not to lie down beside her and take her in his arms again.

And this time, comforting her would have played no part whatever in the way he held her.

Chapter Nine

Through what remained of the night, Ben pondered the reasons why he had chosen not to seduce Phoebe. After all, that was his avowed goal, to seduce her, then toss her out, thereby having his revenge upon her for the pain she had caused him eight years ago.

So why had he not seized this golden opportunity? Considering Phoebe's momentary vulnerability, it would have been so easy to woo her into submission.

Perhaps it was that very vulnerability that stopped him. Or perhaps it was because she had already been mauled about by one man that evening. All Ben knew for certain was that there was a fine line between taking his pleasure where he found it and being a cad, and for some reason he did not wish to examine, he was reluctant to cross that line.

Sleep was impossible, and for a long time Ben watched the fire as it burned itself down, leaving nothing but orange-red embers glowing in the dark gray ashes. Outside, the snow had ceased to fall, and a hush had settled over the world; while inside, the only sound was of Phoebe's soft breathing.

At some point, Ben had regulated his breathing to the pace of hers, but it had proved a mistake. A surprisingly intimate act, it made him all too aware of the woman who slept not ten feet away, in his bed. Knowing how easy it would be to crawl in beside her and pull her soft, yielding body close to his, he strode over to the window, threw aside the heavy drapery, then placed his overheated forehead against the frosted pane.

The coolness brought with it temporary sanity, and when Ben realized that dawn's blue-gray light was already replacing the blackness of the night sky, he deemed it time to return Phoebe to her own bed, before the servants began to stir. It would not do for the maid to find their guest in the master's bed.

His goal was to make Phoebe sorry she had thrown him over; it had never been a part of his plan to ruin her reputation.

Knowing what he must do, he first opened the door. Then he approached the bed, where he slowly rolled back the covers, replacing them with Phoebe's cloak to keep her warm. Lifting her carefully, he carried her down the corridor to her own bedchamber. It was an indication of her fatigue that while in his arms, she did not even stir. Once he laid her on the narrow cot, however, and pulled the covers up over her shoulders, she turned on her side and curled into a ball, both her hands tucked beneath her cheek, almost as if she cuddled a long-forgotten doll.

Ben could only stare, for in that pose, she appeared unbelievably childlike and defenseless, and it brought to mind flashes of vulnerability he had seen in her eight years ago. At that time, he had pushed those insights to the back of his mind, for he had not wished to entertain the idea that the girl he loved might not be the perfect creature he thought her.

Because of his youthful ardor, Ben had been preoccupied with Phoebe's beauty and her joyous nature. She had appeared so carefree, like any other normal young girl enjoying her first Season in town. Now, however, as he looked at her not with the eyes of a love-struck youth, but with the eyes of a man who had seen untold suffering and pain throughout his war years, he recalled those unguarded glimpses of her insecurity.

Phoebe Lowell had been orphaned as a little girl, and no one knew better than Ben what it meant to a child to be alone in the world, or as alone as made no difference. Having no one to count on in their young lives made children needy, and unless those children found someone to love and care for them somewhere along the way—someone whose love would erase the early fears—those needy children grew into equally needy adults.

Fighting a compassion he did not wish to feel, Ben reached down and lifted a lock of hair that had fallen across Phoebe's cheek. Her skin was warm from sleep, and as he smoothed the thick curl back from her face, she sighed.

"Damnation!" he muttered beneath his breath. As if unable to look at her another minute, he turned and strode from the room, closing the door softly behind him, lest he wake her.

For the next two hours, Ben paced the floor of his bedchamber, the door open so he could hear should anyone other than the young maid approach Phoebe's room. When at last he heard Trudy's footfalls, he closed his own door, removed the rather florid robe that had belonged to his uncle, and threw it across the end of the bed with more vehemence than it merited.

He had worn the dressing gown while holding Phoebe in his arms, and the satin lapels still held traces of the clean, womanly fragrance that was so much a part of her. Irritated beyond all reason at himself for not being able to get Phoebe out of his thoughts, he cursed aloud, then he stomped across to the dressing room, lit a candle in one of the wall sconces, and opened the leather box containing his uncle's razors.

Within twenty minutes, Ben was shaved, dressed, and on his way belowstairs to ask a few questions of Abbott and the housekeeper. He meant to discover the identity of the man who had accosted Phoebe, and if that pair of ill-trained servants knew what was good for them, they would be quick with the answers to his questions.

Phoebe was awakened by the homey sounds of someone rebuilding the fire, and for a moment she could not make sense of where she was, or why her cloak was tangled all around her beneath the bed covers. The last time she had seen her cloak, it was on the wall peg. She had taken it down to go belowstairs for a glass of—

Oh, no! The man in the kitchen!

As memory rushed back to her, Phoebe sat up. Ben had carried her to his room. She had slept in his bed. How, and when, had she left it?

"Did you say ought, miss?"

"Trudy!"

"Yes, miss?"

Hoping she had not given voice to her thoughts, Phoebe said, "Your pardon, Trudy. I was merely thinking aloud."

"That's all right, then, miss. Many's a time I've talked to meself, just for the company of it. 'Trudy,' I'd say, 'you'd better get a move on.' Or, 'Trudy, me girl, 'ow would you like a nice walk in the sunshine?'"

"Trudy," Phoebe said, stopping the girl before she could continue with her recitation, "do you know a man who might have been in the kitchen last evening? Tall and slender, about Lord Holden's age?"

The young maid's friendly face turned white as the snow outdoors. "N-no, miss. I don't know nothing about nobody. I swear I don't."

Trudy would never make a whist player, for her

every emotion showed on her face. Mere seconds earlier she had been smiling, but at the question about the stranger in the kitchen, her smile vanished, replaced by a reticence so obvious it would have been comical had the girl not appeared genuinely frightened.

With trembling hands, she returned to the task of lighting the fire. Then, once the flames caught, the girl gathered up her wood basket and her ash bucket and brush. "If that be all, miss, I'll see to the master's fire, then I'll bring up your 'ot water." Not waiting for an answer, she bobbed a curtsy and exited the room as quickly as possible.

While observing the young servant's peculiar behavior, Phoebe decided that one need not be a Bow Street Runner to know that some sort of mischief was afoot in this house. And whatever the nature of that mischief, she would wager her next quarter's earnings it had to do with the furniture missing from the drawing room—the furniture she had seen hidden beneath Holland covers the first night she arrived. As for the man she had bumped into last night, she had no doubt that he was somehow involved.

What his involvement might be, she could not even guess, but she knew without a doubt that the servants were aware of the man's existence and his identity. Not twenty-four hours ago, Mary Abbott had acted every bit as frightened as Trudy just because Phoebe had come down to the kitchen and seen the two extra plates remaining on the table.

Not, of course, that this was any of Phoebe's affair. Holden House belonged to Ben; *she* was but a guest here, and an uninvited guest at that. As a result of the amnesia Ben suffered, he did not even remember her, and he had no reason whatever to trust her. Even so, she considered it her responsibility to tell him what she knew. Once that was done, it was Ben's place to act as he thought best.

As for Phoebe, considering what had happened to her last evening, she would be well advised to keep her nose out of things that did not concern her. All she need do was stay out of the kitchen from now on, and remain in her room at night, with the door locked. It was a good plan. Safe. Sensible.

Having determined her best course of action, she felt immensely better. No longer frightened of a possible second encounter with the unknown man, she decided that what she needed was a breath of fresh air. It had snowed again last night—she knew that from the melting snowflakes on the man's coat—so a long walk was out of the question. She could, however, step just outside the entrance door.

Suiting the action to the thought, Phoebe did not wait for the hot water Trudy promised to bring her; instead, she dressed, twisted her hair into a loose knot at the nape of her neck, then made her way down the stairs and out the double front doors. The instant she stepped outside, she could tell that the worst of the bad weather was over.

The wind that had stung her cheeks and burned her lungs yesterday morning had blown itself out, and yesterday's gray sky had given way to clear blue. In addition, the sun sat firm and yellow just beyond the trees, where it had already begun to melt the icicles that hung from the eaves.

The carriageway, though still several inches deep in snow, was at least discernable, and as if to reiterate that fact, an elderly man dressed in a workman's smock and a brown wool coat appeared from around the end of the house. In his hand he carried a wooden staff, with which he prodded five milk cows—four reddish colored and one black—urging them toward the brick wall at the end of the carriageway.

Around each cow's neck hung a leather thong looped through the eye of a large, square cow bell. Each bell had been painted a bright yellow, with an ox-eye daisy handsomely depicted on the front, but even the pretty flower could not make up for the dull monotone of the five wooden clappers clanking against the tin sides of the bells.

"Good morning," Phoebe called above the clanking.

"Miss," the old man replied, touching the bill of his cap respectfully. If he was surprised to see a stranger standing on the front stoop, he kept his reaction to himself.

"Are you taking the animals for a walk?" Phoebe asked.

"A walk?" The old man lifted his hand to his mouth to hide his smile. "These b'aint hounds, miss."

Phoebe smiled as well, allowing the dairyman his little joke at her expense. "Believe it or not," she said, "we have cows in the city. I merely wondered why they were not in the barn where it was warm."

"I be taking 'em to t'pasture cowshed."

"In this weather? What if it snows again?"

"T'snow be over for the noo, miss, and t'barn be too crowded for 'em."

Country dwellers had a knack for predicting the weather, and Phoebe was delighted to hear that the snowstorms were gone, at least for the next few days.

"Milch cows be skittery around strangers," the dairyman continued. "Let 'em get too skittery, think on, and they'll go dry, wi' nary a drop of milch left for the new master's table."

Assuming the "stranger" the old dairyman referred to was her, Phoebe said no more. However, as she watched him resume his prodding of the cows, urging them past the snow-covered shrubbery, toward the brick wall that bordered the lane, it occurred to her

that he had decided to move the cows *before* he saw
her.

"Sir," she called, raising her voice above the noise
of the clanking bells, "wait, please."

The old man obeyed her request, waiting while
Phoebe picked her way toward him. She moved carefully, hoping to keep the snow out of her boots. "Sir,"
she said once she reached him, "when you—"

"Methias," he said, removing his cap to reveal thick
iron gray hair that stood out in every direction. "What
can I do for ye, miss?"

"You mentioned strangers, Methias, and just last
evening, in the house, I encountered a man who gave
me quite a fright."

The old dairyman's face was unreadable. "Ye don't
say so? I'm that sorry ye were frightened, miss, but it
be an old 'ouse. Mayhap what ye saw were a ghost."

"A ghost," she said, not even trying to hide the
skepticism in her voice.

"Aye, miss. All these old 'ouses got at least one
spirit what refuses to leave the premises."

Exasperated at such nonsense, Phoebe shook her
head. "What you say of old houses may or may not be
true, but I assure you, in this instance the person was
flesh and blood. I collided with him, and he was no
spirit. And, I might add, no gentleman either. Now, if
you will be so good as to answer me with something
other than taradiddles, I should like to know if you
have seen this man. Is he one of the strangers who has
made the cows uneasy?"

The old man cleared his throat, as if stalling for
time in which to think up a suitable reply.

"The truth, if you please, Methias. You have my
word on it, I mean you no harm."

He studied the cap in his hand, not looking at
Phoebe. "I be just an old man, miss. Been tending
t'milch cows at 'Olden 'Ouse nigh on sixty years, and

in that time I glimmed t'secret of not being let go. 'Cept where t'cows be concerned, I keeps me eyes lowered and me mouth shut. That be why I were kept on when them others was let go."

"What others? Do you mean other servants?"

The old man merely shook his head. "I don't see nofing and I don't say nofing, and in return I gets me belly filled daily and me pockets lined with gelt every quarter day."

With that, he placed his cap on his head, touched the bill in polite farewell, then gave his attention once again to the small herd. "Move along there," he called to the bovines, "time be a-wasting."

Phoebe had no recourse but to let the old fellow go. She was certain he knew the identity of the man who had grabbed her last night, but she doubted there was the slightest chance of getting him to reveal what he knew. In his own way, Methias was as frightened as Trudy and Mrs. Abbott were.

Swallowing her frustration, Phoebe watched quietly while the cows lumbered down the curved carriageway, past a stand of snow-covered trees, and continued to the entrance gates. In no time they had disappeared down the lane. Once the dissonant clanking of their bells had faded into the distance, Phoebe turned and retraced her steps back through the snow to the front stoop, no wiser than she had been before she spoke to the old dairyman.

During the few minutes Phoebe spent out-of-doors in fruitless conversation with Methias, Ben stood in the kitchen concluding an equally unproductive questioning of Henry and Mary Abbott. To Ben's annoyance, the butler could not even stand upon his feet. Unshaven and bleary-eyed, the man slouched across the refectory table, holding his head in his hands, apparently far too touched by the potent juice of Bacchus to do more than groan in response to Ben's questions. In regard to the man who had been in the kitchen last night, Abbott either could not or would not identify him.

"And what of you?" Ben asked, turning quickly to glare at the white-faced housekeeper.

"Me, my lord?"

"Yes, you. What can you tell me of this man who enters my house without so much as a word of invitation from me?"

"Nothing, my lord. I . . . I'm a sound sleeper, and if anyone entered the house without leave to do so, I'm sure I cannot say who it might've been."

"Can you not?" Ben asked. "And why, I wonder, am I having so much trouble believing you?"

The woman began to cry, and when she raised her apron to cover her face, Ben decided he had heard all he was likely to hear for the moment. With the butler too jug-bitten to form an intelligent sentence, and the housekeeper turning into a watering pot, obviously more frightened of the mysterious interloper than she was of her new employer, Ben came to the conclusion that he was wasting his time here.

"Be warned," he added, his temper only just held in check, "I shall get to the bottom of this. And, if the mysterious intruder should show his face inside my house again, he will find he has more to contend with than a young lady."

Mary Abbott's only reply was a renewal of her sobs.

Having issued his warning, Ben turned and strode from the room. Not that he was finished with his interrogation—not by a long shot. He was determined to discover what was going on in this house, but it was obvious he would get nowhere at the moment, not with that disreputable pair in the kitchen.

He could ask Aunt Constance, of course, but he was loath to do so. She was an elderly lady, and the idea that a strange man was roaming the premises might well frighten her into a decline.

Barring that venue, he made up his mind to have a look around the barn and the other outbuildings later that day to see if he could find any clues as to what was going on inside his house. In the mean time, he would write a letter to Mr. McNeese, his uncle's solicitor, demanding to know what sort of servants the fellow thought suitable for a gentleman's establishment. Certainly, the Abbotts did not fit *his* definition of a competent pair.

The letter in mind, Ben headed for the library. As he passed through the empty drawing room, however, he happened to glance out one of the front-facing windows, and to his surprise, he spied Phoebe standing in the carriageway, staring out toward the lane. Upon seeing her there, all else was pushed from his thoughts, for it occurred to Ben that his bogus fiancée might be trying her luck at fleeing the house.

Not that he blamed her. At the moment, he could offer her none of the amenities a lady might reasonably expect while a guest in a peer's home, and considering the fright she sustained last evening in the kitchen, she probably wanted nothing so much as to get away.

And, of course, there was the matter of his dotty aunt. Let Phoebe say what she would about Constance Holden being just a sweet old lady who clings to the past; in truth, his aunt was touched in her upper works. Any normal woman, even one who might have harbored hopes of becoming mistress of the house, could be forgiven for having second thoughts about joining such a family.

"Let her go," he muttered, "and be damned to her! What do I care if she leaves?"

The words had no sooner left his mouth than Ben turned and hurried to the vestibule. He told himself that his urgency stemmed from his not wanting to be robbed of his chance for revenge upon Phoebe, and though he searched his brain for some plausible excuse to keep her at Holden House at least one more day, he still had not come up with anything remotely convincing when he swung open the heavy entrance doors.

To his surprise, he very nearly collided with her, for she had just stepped up onto the stoop.

"Ben!"

"Phoebe," he said, grabbing her arms to steady her, "I thought—"

He stopped himself just in time, for Phoebe's lips had parted in a smile, and unless he much mistook the light in her eyes, she was pleased to see him.

"Good morning, Ben. Is it not a beautiful day?"

Too dumbfounded to speak, he merely nodded.

"I collect, sir, that you and I were of similar minds, that with the storm over and the sun out, a breath of fresh air was in order."

Fresh air? Was that her reason for going outside?

More than happy to let her continue in the misguided belief that his purpose was as innocent as hers, he said, "I must confess, ma'am, that when I saw you on the carriageway, it occurred to me that you and I might be of like minds. In which instance, I should like to suggest an outing that would be far more salubrious than slogging through the snow, getting your feet cold and your hems sodden."

Her smile widened. "You see me positively agog with interest. Make your suggestion by all means."

"If memory serves me," he said, "there is an old sleigh in the stables, and—" He stopped abruptly, all but choking on the words, for Phoebe's smile had vanished, and she looked at him with eyes that had grown wide with surprise.

Deuce take it! This amnesia business was a blasted nuisance.

As if to cover his gaffe, he feigned a cough, making much of pounding his chest, as though to aid in catching his breath. "What I should have said was that *Trudy* thought there might be such a sleigh. My idea was to ascertain if such a vehicle really exists, and if it does, to have a horse put to it this very morning. After we have broken our fasts, of course."

During his rather hurried speech, Phoebe had watched him, as if not certain what to think. And while she stared, the skin just above the bridge of her nose crinkled as if she tried to make sense of something too preposterous to credit. Fortunately, by the time Ben had finished his explanation, her smile, though tentative, was back in place.

"What say you, ma'am, shall I have Trudy bring a meal for two to the library?"

"The library, is it? I might have known you would choose that room."

"Would you prefer another?"

"Oh, not at all." She sighed dramatically, giving the lie to her denial. "I pray you, sir, do not concern yourself with my preferences, for I will not have it said that Phoebe Lowell is an uncooperative guest."

Ben chuckled, pleased to see that her playful mood had returned. "Madam, the word *uncooperative* never entered my mind. If the truth be known, I am amazed at your continued forbearance. Considering the disreputable state of this house, not to mention the noticeable ineptness of the servants, I would say you have exhibited an exceptional degree of tolerance."

Phoebe felt her face grow warm at the unexpected compliment. "And if my tolerance, as you call it, should lead me to agree to join you in the library, have I your solemn oath, my lord, that I need not share my repast with the polar bear?"

She had expected him to laugh again, but he did not, though the light in his eyes told her he was amused. "You need share with no one but me," he replied softly. "Only with me."

"If that is the case, then I accept your invitation."

"And the sleigh ride?"

A few seconds ago, Phoebe had been unable to hide her pleasure at seeing Ben in the doorway. Now, she made no effort to conceal her delight at his suggestion they go for a drive in the snow. "If such a vehicle does, indeed, exist, I should love to ride in it."

"Wonderful. There is that forbearance again. Now run up and warm yourself by your fire, there's a good girl, while I order the meal. Then join me again when you are ready. In half an hour, say?"

While Ben saw to the ordering of the meal, Phoebe ran up to her bedchamber to leave her cloak and to warm her hands and feet before the fire. She would have loved to put on something other than the sadly crushed pale blue merino she had been wearing since Saturday, but that was not possible. Telling herself there was nothing to be gained by fretting over things that could not be helped, she washed her face, re-combed her hair, and draped about her neck a lace fichu lent to her by Miss Constance.

Feeling slightly more presentable, Phoebe returned belowstairs and made her way to the library. Ben was already there, leaning against the carved oak mantel, and he looked so relaxed and so handsome that at least a hundred butterflies began to flit about inside Phoebe's midsection.

A fire had been lit in the grate, and the fledgling flames were beginning to take the chill out of the air. As for the room, it had been dusted and tidied up since last evening, and with the fire going, it promised to be a most inviting retreat.

"Has this your approval?" Ben asked. He motioned toward the polar bear rug, which someone had placed before the hearth, stretched out between the gold brocade settee and the tan leather wing chair.

Thankfully, the massive head was pointed toward the fireplace, away from Phoebe, so that she need not look at the long, yellow teeth. As for the remainder of the animal, the thick white fur contrasted handsomely with the muted reds and blues of the worn turkey carpet, and the effect was both luxurious and inviting.

"In the light of day," Phoebe said, her gaze moving from the bear's head back up to Ben's face, "the fellow appears not at all ferocious. In fact, he seems rather tame."

Ben's lips twitched at the corners. "Madam, you cannot know how fervently I pray that the fellow to whom you refer is the polar bear and not me."

Phoebe did not attempt to hide her laughter. "There is an old adage, my lord, that says if one would not be lied to, one should ask no questions."

Though Ben did not laugh, his brown eyes sparkled with merriment. "There is an even older adage, one that warns saucy females to beware making sport of a gentleman who has not yet broken his fast."

"Oh? And why is that?"

"The answer, madam, is obvious, for said hungry gentleman might be tempted to eat said saucy female instead."

"Ha! You do not frighten me, Ben Holden."

"No?" he asked very softly.

"Not the least little bit."

The flippant statement, which sounded very like a dare, prompted Ben to push away from the mantel and take a step toward her. The sudden, unexpected movement seemed to accentuate his height and the breadth of his shoulders, and as he drew nearer, stopping mere inches from her, Phoebe felt a frisson of excitement skitter up her spine.

"I shall not eat you," he said, his gaze concentrated upon her mouth, "but I find myself unable to resist a little nibble."

Phoebe felt her breath catch in her throat, and when Ben looked up at her, the passion she saw shining in his dark eyes routed those hundred flitting butterflies from her midsection, leaving in their place a sudden heat that coursed through her entire body, threatening to consume her. Startled by the power of that heat, Phoebe took a step back, putting space between herself and Ben.

He meant to kiss her, and Heaven help her, she wanted to be kissed. Unfortunately, while he had held her gaze, Phoebe had been struck by a sudden realization—a realization so earth shattering that she was obliged to reach her hand toward the bookshelf, seeking something substantial to lean upon.

She was in love with Ben Holden.

Chapter Ten

Phoebe loved Ben Holden. She loved him with all her heart. Perhaps she had never stopped loving him.

And yet, the girlish emotions she had experienced eight years ago were but pale imitations of the burning need she felt at this moment. This new feeling, this desire, was so strong that the mere thought of Ben touching her, of him kissing her as he so obviously meant to do, caused her entire body to tremble.

"Pretty one," he whispered when she stepped back, "would you deny me a small taste of your sweet—" He stopped in mid-sentence, his attention moving from her face down to her trembling hands. "Phoebe! What is amiss?"

"Nothing, I just—"

"Deuce take it, I am an idiot! I completely forgot about that cur in the kitchen last evening. No wonder you retreated. Forgive me. And please, I beg of you, do not mistake me for that blackguard who forced his attentions upon you."

Catching her hand, he spoke more softly. "I hope you know I would never do anything of that nature. When you come to me, my pretty one, it will be of your own free will, or not at all."

Before Phoebe could disabuse Ben of the notion that he had frightened her, or erase from her own mind the foolish, heart-stopping idea that she might come to him—free will or not—there was a knock at the library door.

"Begging your lordship's pardon," Trudy said from the doorway, "but I've brought the tray. Where you want I should set it?"

"Here," Ben replied calmly, drawing up a small occasional table beside the hearth. "And thank you, Trudy, for your arrival was well timed."

And not a minute too soon. No, Phoebe corrected herself, her heart still pounding as though someone were using it for a drum, not a *second* too soon.

How it came about that they sat on the bearskin rug, Phoebe could not seem to remember, but while they partook of basted eggs, thinly sliced ham, and currant buns, Ben talked of inconsequential things, entertaining her with tales of the Frost Fair held on the Thames during the first week in February. Never once did he refer to what had passed between them before Trudy arrived with their meal, and when they had finished their repast, he returned the used plates to the tray, while Phoebe poured cups of fragrant Bohea.

"Sitting like this," she said, passing him one of the lovely blue-and-gold bone china cups, "puts me in mind of an impromptu picnic we once shared in green park."

"Oh?" Ben leaned his back against the arm of the tan leather wing chair, and after taking a sip of the warm tea, he said, "Pray continue, Scheherazade, for you find me quite eager to hear the story."

Phoebe took a sip from her cup. Then she set it down and made herself more comfortable, tucking the hem of her dress around her ankles, which she had drawn up beside her. "On that particular occasion," she began, "Miss Barrington—"

"Your confounded chaperone."

"My *indisposed* chaperone," she corrected, "was laid upon her bed with the headache, poor dear, so instead of driving to Richmond, which was our original destination, we decided to walk to Green Park."

She smiled, as if enjoying the memory. "Before we entered the park," she continued, "you purchased meat pasties from a pieman in Piccadilly. Then later, after we had walked among the trees, where uniformed nursemaids pushed wicker prams and watched over children who played with balls and hoops, we sat on the greensward and ate our humble meal like a pair of Gypsies." Phoebe sighed. "It was a delightful day."

"Yes, it was. That is to say, it *sounds* quite delightful."

As it happened, Ben remembered every minute of that particular day, for it was during that afternoon in Green Park that he realized he loved Phoebe Lowell and wished to spend the rest of his life with her. Furthermore, on more than one occasion during those long, painful days in Portugal, while he waited to be shipped home to England, he had eased the unrelenting pain from his wound by recalling their simple picnic.

It had been the last week in April, and a bed of daffodils had just begun to show a hint of yellow. He and Phoebe had eaten their pasties beneath the branches of a newly leafed beech tree, and because they were young, and the day was gloriously sunny, they had laughed at everything and at nothing.

One of their amusements had come in the form of a pair of combative hares seen in the distance. The long-eared animals were engaged in battle over a female who munched grass nearby, apparently ignoring them. Standing on their hind legs, the pair boxed, their small, furry paws jabbing quickly, in a one-two, one-two motion. For the most part, neither hare hit anything more than air, but occasionally one of those paws connected with the opponent's head or body with such force that the unlucky hare was knocked over.

"Show him your science," Ben had yelled, pretending he and Phoebe were witnessing a mill featuring celebrated pugilists. "That's the dandy!" he said once the fallen hare was again up on his hind legs. "This time give him a right to the jaw."

"My money is on the hare to the left," Phoebe said, joining in the fun.

"Save your blunt, Miss Lowell, for my man, the one on the right, has all the science. I fear your fellow is all Lancaster Method."

"Though I have not the least idea what any of that boxing cant means, Lieutenant, I recognize an insult when I hear one, and I am not above a bit of battling myself." After a moment's consideration, she added, "A shilling says my man proves victorious. What say you, Lieutenant Holden? Do you care to match my bet?"

Though Ben had been unable to keep from laughing, he felt it his duty not to let the conversation get out of hand. "Ladies do not wager on such things as mills, Miss Lowell, even pastoral ones, and if your uncle should hear that I had introduced you to such unacceptable—"

"Stuff and nonsense, sir. Match my shilling, or I shall feel it my duty to spread it about town that you are a . . . a flat."

Pretending to be scandalized at her use of such unladylike jargon, Ben said, "Madam! Pray, what do you know of flats?"

"I know they are not sharps," she retorted.

"As a gently reared young lady, may I assume you are speaking of music?"

"You may assume nothing of the sort. And I beg of you, do not attempt to divert my attention from the subject at hand. Do you accept my wager or do you not?"

Ben had been hard pressed at that moment not to take the lovely girl in his arms and kiss her full, smiling lips. "A shilling it is," he said.

The words had only just left his mouth when Ben's "man" took another telling blow to the head and fell backward. With a high-pitched squeal, the hare righted himself, then fled with all haste, running for the safety of some nearby shrubbery.

"Ah ha!" Phoebe shouted. "I told you how it would be. Just look at your man run."

"Come back here, you cawker! The fight is not over yet."

"It is," Phoebe said, holding out her gloved hand. "My winnings, if you please, Lieutenant."

As he searched his uniform for the shilling, Ben noticed a young boy, perhaps four years of age, run from his nursemaid, apparently under the misguided belief that he could catch the fleeing hare.

"Master William," the plump, gray-haired woman called to her charge. "Have a care, for there is a pond behind the shrubbery."

When the little boy paid her no heed, but continued to pursue the hare, the servant panicked. "Master William!" she yelled, waking the pink-blanketed infant who slept in her arms. "Master William! Come back!"

While the woman screamed, the baby let out a series of kitten-like mews of protest, whereupon the small dog, who accompanied them became excited and began to jump about, echoing his own objections with high-pitched *yip, yip, yip!*

Within a matter of seconds, two more dogs had joined the canine chorus, and other nursemaids were anxiously calling for their own charges to come to the safety of their arms.

Not waiting for further pandemonium to break out, Ben set off at a run to fetch the four-year-old who had now reached the shrubbery, sending the victorious hare and his previously unconcerned light-o-love scurrying for cover.

Fortunately, with his much longer legs, Ben overtook the adventurous lad before he came to harm, scooping him up into his arms just as he reached the shrubbery. "Sorry, youngster, but it is unlawful to course hares in the park. Would you settle for a horsie ride instead?"

Not the least bit afraid, the boy nodded enthusiastically.

"Good choice." After swinging the lad up onto his shoulders, Ben galloped back across the greensward toward the nursemaid, an action that soon turned the child's thoughts from hares to horses.

"Go, sir!" the happy rider urged, pretending to use a crop on the two-legged equine.

The nursemaid was so relieved to see her precocious charge unharmed, and on his way back to her, that she shoved the crying infant into Phoebe's arms and rushed to meet Ben. Moments later, she gathered the little boy to her more-than-ample bosom and hugged him until he cried out that he could not breathe.

Ben, too, received a hug from the grateful woman, and afterward he was obliged to endure embarrassingly protracted expressions of her gratitude. By the time he was able to extricate himself and return to Phoebe, the excitement was over and both dogs and children had resumed their earlier, quieter pursuits. Even the infant had ceased its kittenlike protests and was nestled contentedly in Phoebe's arms.

As for Phoebe, she held the small, pink-blanketed babe with a mixture of tenderness and awe, as though it were some sort of magical creature. With her lovely face nuzzled against the small, downy head, she cooed soft nonsense to the baby. To Ben's surprise, Phoebe's eyes were closed, as if to heighten her senses, and when he spoke her name, she looked up slowly, reluctantly.

Gentleness filled her soft, gray-green eyes, reminding Ben of a painting of the Madonna and Child, and as he gazed at Phoebe and the babe, something grabbed hold of his heart, squeezing it until he thought it might never beat normally again. Bereft of speech, he merely stared, and in that instant he realized that he loved Phoebe Lowell with all his soul, and that he would continue to love her for eternity.

"I am truly sorry," Phoebe said, bringing Ben's thoughts back to the present, and to the cup of tea that had grown cold in his hand, "that you have no memory of our picnic in Green Park."

"I am sorry as well," he whispered, "for it sounds like a wonderful day."

Following the breakfast, which had turned out to be a most pleasant experience, Ben waited until Phoebe had climbed the circular staircase to visit his Aunt Constance, then he hurried up to his bedchamber to possess himself of his pocket pistol and his greatcoat. Upon his return belowstairs, he crossed the vestibule to the paneled room on the right. Moving directly to the fireplace, he pushed a button hidden beneath the gray slate mantelpiece, then waited while a door concealed in the paneling swung open.

Using the secret exit, he quit the house, his objective to have a look-in at the stables. Walking as quickly as the snow would allow, he had covered half the distance of the stable yard when the kitchen door flew open, the thick wood banging against the wall with a loud thud. An instant later, Abbott came running toward him, though what his intention might be, Ben could only guess.

Drink and indolence had taken their toll on the butler, and before he had covered fifty feet, he was wheezing like a bellows. "My lord," he said, his breath coming in gasps, and the pain in his bloodshot eyes revealing all too clearly what running had done to his aching head, "can I be of service to your lordship?"

If Ben had not already had his suspicious about what, or who, he might find in the stables, the butler's sudden appearance would have started him wondering. As it was, he was now convinced that he was on the right track. "Miss Lowell and I wish to go for a ride," he said, sticking with a portion of the truth, "and I wanted to see if that old sleigh was still usable."

"The sleigh?" Abbot said, speaking noticeably louder than was necessary. "Yes, sir, it's usable. Even so, b'aint no need for your lordship to go inside. The stables ain't 'ad a good cleaning in I don't know when, and there's dust and grime everywhere. Like as not, your lordship'll ruin his fine clothes. You don't need to bother yourself about nothing, sir. Just leave all to me. I'll see to everything. You can count on 'Enry Abbott, you can."

Ben had reached the stable door, and when he stretched out his hand to lift the latch, Abbott looked as though he contemplated throwing himself against the wood to bar the new owner's way. He must have thought better of such rash behavior, for he contented himself with another over-loud reassurance of service.

"I'll be 'appy to see to that sled for your lordship," he shouted. "I'll wipe it off so there b'aint a speck of dust on it, sir, then soon as the 'orse is put to, I'll bring the sleigh round front."

After noting the sweat that had popped out on the

butler's forehead, never mind the cold air and the fact that the fellow had come outside in his shirtsleeves, Ben stepped forward and took hold of the latch. To his surprise, it would not lift. "Damnation, Abbot! Why is this door locked?"

"Locked, my lord? I'm sure I don't understand what you mean, sir."

The look of relief on the servant's face was almost comical, and had Ben not been so angry at being thwarted, he might have laughed. "It is bolted from the inside."

"Bolted, you say? I'm that sorry, sir. Wonder 'ow that 'appened."

The butler's relief was followed by a rather cocky smirk, one Ben would have enjoyed knocking off the overgrown lout's face.

"If your lordship will be so good as to return to the 'ouse, I'll see can I find a way into the stables so I can open the door. After that, I'll dust the sleigh and bring it around to the front in two shakes."

The idea of finding an ax and breaking down the door crossed Ben's mind, only to be cast aside. For the moment, he was obliged to admit defeat, but if there was one thing he had learned from his years in the military, it was that there was more than one way to lay siege to a fort. Furthermore, if someone was hiding inside the stable, which Ben felt certain was the case, there was no longer the least chance of taking the fellow by surprise. Much better to wait until later.

"Very well," Ben said, stepping away from the door, "I will expect to see the sleigh within half an hour's time."

"Yes, my lord. Anything you say, my lord."

*   *   *

"Hello," Phoebe called once she reached the landing just outside Constance Holden's bedchamber. "May I come in, ma'am?"

"Please do, my dear. I have been hoping you would come to see me this morning."

"Indeed?" Phoebe said, stepping inside the room, "and why is that, ma'am?"

The elderly lady sat in a slipper chair pulled up beside the window, an untouched breakfast tray on the footstool beside her. Although it was mid-morning, she still wore her night rail, with a lace nightcap tied beneath her wrinkled chin. She looked quite different without her powdered wig and her finery: older somehow, more fragile. Her thin, gray hair was caught in a braid that hung down her back, and her face was free of both powder and patch. And unless Phoebe was mistaken, Miss Constance had been crying.

"My dear girl," the lady said, holding out a trembling hand, "I have something most disturbing to tell you."

Phoebe approached and took the frail hand in hers. "What is amiss, ma'am?"

"It is my Jamie."

Not certain she had heard correctly, Phoebe said, "Do you mean Jamie Whitcombe, your—"

"My beloved fiancé." Miss Constance's bottom lip quivered. "Jamie is dead. All these years I have waited, all the time hoping he would return to me, and now I discover that he is dead—that he was probably dead the entire time."

For a moment, Phoebe was at a loss for words. The elderly lady was obviously distraught, but how did one offer words of comfort to someone who had not seen their beloved in sixty years? And now that she thought of it, how did the news of Jamie's death arrive?

"Miss Constance?" she asked, feeling just a bit foolish, "did you finally receive a letter?"

"A letter?" As if irritated by the question, she said, "Of course not. Use your brains, child. How could anyone deliver the post in this weather?"

"Very true. Forgive me then, ma'am, but how do you know that Jamie is no longer alive?"

"I saw him."

"You saw—"

"Or to be accurate, I saw his ghost."

Not more ghosts! Phoebe had heard just about enough of those discontented specters. Especially since every unpleasant occurrence at Holden House seemed to be laid at their door.

"Miss Constance, I thought you told me it was your brother's ghost that walked the corridors here."

"I did say that, my dear, but apparently I was mistaken. It was not Roland after all. The ghost is my Jamie."

Though losing all patience with this nonsense, Phoebe tried to curb her irritation. "And how did you arrive at that conclusion?"

"I saw him. Jamie, I mean." She pointed out the window. "He was at the door to the stables."

Phoebe looked to where the lady pointed, and to her surprise, she spied Ben just outside the stables, apparently in conversation with Henry Abbott. Ben had his hand in the pocket of his greatcoat, and though his face appeared relaxed enough, his stance told a different story. If she knew anything of the matter, Ben was angry enough to do the servant bodily harm.

"That is not Jamie Whitcombe, ma'am. It is your nephew."

"Not now," Miss Constance said, annoyance in her tone, "pray, do not treat me like some demented old fool. Jamie was there earlier."

As if in answer to Phoebe's unvoiced doubts, she added, "He turned and looked up toward my window, and I saw him clearly. His face was just as I remembered it."

Tears spilled down the elderly lady's cheeks, but she brushed them aside with an impatient hand. "That is how I know that he died many years ago. The ghost's face is just as I remembered it, still youthful looking."

"I am afraid I do not see the connect—"

"Jamie would be eighty-four now," she said, as if obliged to explain the obvious to one lacking in good sense. "The only way his ghost would have a youthful face is if my Jamie had died young."

Phoebe ignored that pseudo logic and pursued a far more interesting piece of information—the fact that Miss Constance had seen her supposed ghost out-of-doors and not in some dark corner of the house. The man who had attacked Phoebe last evening had come from the outside. "I wonder," she said, more to herself that to Miss Constance, "at what time this sighting occurred."

"Actually, my dear, I have seen him twice, though I did not recognize him on the first occasion. It was still dark out at that time, don't you know."

"Still dark?"

"That is correct. I saw him for the first time last night. Like most elderly people, I am a light sleeper, and at some time between midnight and dawn I was awakened by what I thought was a scream."

Phoebe's skepticism vanished, replaced on the instant by avid interest. "You say you heard a scream?"

"I said I 'thought' it was a scream. After thinking the matter through, however, I believe I was mistaken. Now, I am persuaded it was an owl I heard. You must know," she added, "that the hoot of an owl is often an omen from the other side."

Phoebe did not dignify that bit of folklore with a response; instead, she removed the untouched breakfast tray, pulled the stool close to the elderly lady's chair, then seated herself. "After you were awakened, ma'am, what did you do?"

"Earlier in the evening, I had thought I heard someone walking about in the stable yard. I could not be certain, though, for the snow all but deadened the sound of the footfalls. After the owl hooted, however, I came over here by the window where I could look out. That was when I saw the ghost for the first time, hurrying across the yard."

"Hurrying?"

"To be more accurate, he *tried* to hurry. Unfortunately, he was bent over, as if he were hurt. When he reached the stable door, he did not turn around, but slipped inside and shut the door quickly. Even so, I got a reasonably good look at him."

"Then you saw only his back?"

She nodded. "But even though I did not see his face last night, something about him made me think it might be Jamie. That is why I remained here."

"Ma'am, never tell me you have been sitting in that chair since last night."

"Naturally I have. Had I returned to my bed, I would not have seen my Jamie again this morning. Less than an hour ago, he came out of the stables again. Only this time, he peeped out first, as if afraid someone might see him. He looked up, toward my window, and I saw his face clearly in the sunlight."

"You are quite certain, ma'am?"

"Oh, yes. He has changed very little. That is, with one exception. Though Jamie still carries himself in a tall and commanding manner, he is considerably thinner than when I saw him last. I suppose he lost weight while fighting the French and Indians in the colonies, which is probably why he no longer wears his uniform."

As if to lend credence to her supposition, she held up her hand to display the ring on her finger. "Truth to tell, I have lost some weight myself. When Jamie put his grandmother's ring on my finger, it was a bit snug. Now, as you can see, it is forever slipping."

Just as she said, the small ruby set in the center of the thin gold band had twisted all the way to the inside of her hand. Not that Phoebe had the least interest in some old ring. She wanted to hear more about the supposed ghost.

Miss Constance sighed. "Jamie always looked so splendid in his red coat."

Keeping her voice calm, Phoebe said, "Did you notice, ma'am, what he was wearing in place of the uniform?"

"Naturally I noticed. He wore a dark driving coat and light-colored breeches."

Phoebe bit her lip to keep from voicing her suspicions regarding the identity of the far-from-otherworldly man Miss Constance had seen enter the stables last evening. After a full minute of silence, she turned her attention to the elderly lady herself, suggesting that she might wish to return to her bed. "If you have been awake since last night, you must be in need of a nap."

"I am sleepy, my dear. In fact, I found myself nodding off a little while ago. I may already have missed Jamie's return to the stables."

"I would not be at all surprised, ma'am."

"And," Miss Constance added, "I am painfully stiff from having sat in one place for too long. Do you think you could help me to my feet?"

"Of course, ma'am."

Phoebe put her hand beneath the lady's elbow and helped her to stand. "Come," she said, holding her while they walked her over to the bed, then helping her to climb beneath the covers.

Almost as soon as Constance Holden's head touched the pillows, she fell asleep, and by the time Phoebe had tiptoed to the landing, gentle snores were filling the room.

After she left the apartment, Phoebe hurried down the spiral stairs, then ran up the broad marble staircase to her bedchamber, where she fetched her cloak. Within minutes, she was on the move again, hurrying back down to the library.

"Ben," she said, finding him once again beside the fireplace, "I just come from visiting Miss Constance, and in a million years, you will not guess what she just told me."

When Ben said nothing, Phoebe continued. "Your great-aunt saw a man in the stable yard last evening, and she believes him to be the ghost of Jamie Whitcombe, her long-lost fiancé!"

Chapter Eleven

Ben let out an audible breath. Knowing Aunt Constance, she might have told Phoebe anything. A number of possible revelations had come to his mind, not the least of which was the existence of the letter of condolence he had written to his great-aunt following the death of her brother Roland—a letter that would have revealed Ben's amnesia as a hoax.

Happy to know that the remaining member of the "dotty trio" had done no more than admit to seeing the ghost of her erstwhile fiancé, Ben breathed a sigh relief.

Touching his finger to his lips, to silence Phoebe temporarily, he took the cloak from her hands and draped it around her shoulders. "Come," he said, "I believe I heard Abbott bringing the sleigh around, and since I do not trust the man, I suggest you say no more until we are away from the house. You can tell me everything while we ride."

Phoebe nodded her agreement. Waiting only until Ben had grabbed up his greatcoat and beaver hat, along with a woolen blanket Trudy had fetched to put over their laps, she preceded him from the library. Ben followed her through the adjoining rooms to the vestibule, and out the entrance doors, where the sleigh and horse awaited their pleasure.

The early afternoon sun shone even brighter than before, promising a pleasant ride, and true to his word, Abbott had dusted off the sleigh's black leather seat and back. The woven-cane sides showed definite wear, but the vehicle appeared sturdy enough, with both runners in good condition. As for the horse hitched to the sleigh, it was the same dappled gray Ben had hired at the inn in Shrewsbury—a fact that told its own story about the possibility of decent horseflesh in the stables.

The butler stood at the animal's head, his face turned away, and while he held the bridle with his right hand, he stuffed his left hand beneath his right arm pit in an attempt to keep it warm. Still in his shirtsleeves, the servant shivered so badly his teeth chattered.

"As your-r-r lor-r-rdship r-r-requested," he said.

Ben helped Phoebe into the seat, tucked the blanket around her lap, then walked around the sleigh to climb aboard himself. He had just taken up the reins when he heard her gasp. "Abbott," she said, "what on earth happened to your face?"

"B'aint nothing," he replied. "I fell is all."

He ducked his head, but not quickly enough to keep Ben from spying a trickle of blood at the corner of the man's surly mouth and a bruise already turning blue on the side of his face.

He fell right enough—directly against someone's fists!

Though convinced now that the person who had attacked Phoebe was hiding in the stables, Ben kept his thoughts to himself. Besides, he wanted nothing said within Abbott's hearing. Lacing the ribbons between his fingers, he told the butler to step away from the horse's head.

The moment the servant complied, Ben gave the gray the office to be on his way. After an initial lurch forward, the sleigh glided smoothly down the snow-covered carriageway. Once they reached the entrance gates, Ben turned the horse to the right, then encouraged him to continue alongside the low brick wall that snaked its way for perhaps a quarter mile along the gently sloping lane.

An intelligent driver, as well as a skillful one, Ben gave his full attention to the handling of the ribbons until he grew accustomed to the noticeable difference between traveling by wheel and traveling by runner. Finally, when he was certain he had both horse and sleigh under control, he told Phoebe she might tell him about her visit with his great-aunt.

"I will spare you any roundaboutation," she said, "and come right to the point. Miss Constance heard me scream last evening, and following the scream—which she believes was the hoot of an owl—she went to the window, where she saw the ghost of her missing fiancé, Lieutenant Jamie Whitcombe, enter the stables."

After Phoebe had apprised Ben of the entire conversation, she concluded with her own belief, that the supposed *ghost* was no ghost at all, but the man who had accosted her in the kitchen.

"I do not doubt it," Ben said. "In fact, I am certain of it, just as I am certain that the fellow is holed up in the stables as we speak, and that he is responsible for the sorry state of Henry Abbott's face."

"You think he hit the butler? But Abbott must outweigh the man I saw by several stone."

"Perhaps the fellow has an accomplice."

Considering the six dirty plates Phoebe had seen on the kitchen table, an accomplice made sense. "I probably should have told you this earlier, but yesterday morning, when I went to the kitchen, the table was set with two extra plates."

"And?" Ben prompted.

"And though six people had broken their fasts, both Trudy and Methias, the dairyman, insist there are only the four servants on the premises. Of course,

I acquit Trudy and Methias of being anything more than innocent bystanders, but I am persuaded the same cannot be said for the Abbotts."

"I agree. In all probability, my butler and his wife are linked somehow with our mysterious visitors."

"But if they are friends, why would they want to beat poor Abbott?"

"I cannot be certain, but my guess is that it has something to do with the fact that I very nearly entered the stables. And though Abbott tried to stop me with his spurious wishes to be of service to me, I was not fooled. There is something in the stables, something important enough that they bolted the door to keep me from discovering it. Something *other* than your attacker."

"So you already suspected the man was hiding there?"

Ben nodded. "I had surmised as much. However, I cannot begin to guess what he, or anyone else, would find of value at Holden House. Whatever it is, he obviously believes I would stop him from taking it; and chances are, he is correct."

Recalling her vow to tell Ben about the furniture missing from the drawing room—the furniture she had seen hidden beneath Holland covers the first night she arrived—Phoebe said, "Could it be the missing furnishings?"

Ben's reaction was not at all what she expected, and if Phoebe had been asked what she thought, she would have said that he was embarrassed at the mention of the furniture. That was pure nonsense, of course. Why should the new Baron Holden be embarrassed? Especially when he had no memory of either his family or the house as it once looked.

"What furnishings?" he asked at last.

Phoebe told him what she had seen the night of her arrival at Holden House. "And," she added, "the next morning, when I found the room empty, I heard strange noises behind the wall panels. Call me foolish if you will, but I now believe someone was back there."

"There are many things I might call you," Ben said quietly, "but foolish is not one of them."

He said no more, and Phoebe was left to make what she would of his remark. She did not ask for an explanation. She was beginning to understand Ben Holden a little better, and for some reason he did not like to be questioned. It was almost as if he saw questions as a vote of no confidence. He expected, even dared a person to accept him on his own terms, or else leave him alone.

Aided by the clarity of hindsight, Phoebe realized that Ben had embraced that same credo eight years ago.

Unbidden, a picture invaded her thoughts—a picture of Ben as he had looked the day he proposed marriage, the day she refused his offer, calling him a rake. In one breath she had called him a womanizer; then, in another breath she had all but begged him to deny the accusation. Overcome by her own insecurity, yet loving him with all her heart, she had entreated Ben to tell her that the rumors were untrue, and that her uncle was mistaken.

Very young, and very frightened, Phoebe had waited, nearly choking on her own misery, waited for Ben to reassure her that she could trust in his love. He had said nothing, apparently waiting for some show of faith from her. Unfortunately, at that time she had little faith to give.

She remembered a long silence; after which, Ben's eyes—those dark orbs that had always looked upon her with tenderness and warmth—had turned icy cold, chilling her to the very core of her being.

"I never explain," Ben had said. "One either takes me on faith, or one does not."

Recalling that day, Phoebe might have been tempted to laugh, if the circumstances had not been so pathetic. What a pair they had been—an insecure young girl who needed constant reassurance, and a prideful young man who would not justify his actions. No wonder they had been unable to resolve their differences.

Phoebe, orphaned at an early age, had needed to hear him say that he would never leave her for another. She could not understand why, if he truly loved her, he would not want to answer all her questions, to calm all her fears. It was fate's little joke that she had sought reassurance from the one man who, for whatever reasons, needed total acceptance, no questions asked.

She sighed now, realizing that her insight into their respective personalities had come eight years too late. Furthermore, merely understanding a problem did not solve it.

For her part, Phoebe was much stronger now; far less emotionally needy. The hardships of the intervening years, coupled with the discovery that she could support herself, had given her the confidence to trust in her own resources. Coming to terms with the fact that there was no one else she could depend on had forced her to learn to trust in herself.

No longer a naive girl, she did not expect some armor-clad knight to ride into her life on a white horse—some all-powerful male who would act as a buffer between her and the hardships of life. Such unrealistic expectations had faded with her growing maturity. And yet, Phoebe still longed for someone to love her. The problem was that after seeing Ben Holden again, and realizing that she loved him and him alone, she did not want some anonymous "some-one" to love her. She wanted *Ben*.

Unfortunately, in view of the insurmountable differences in their present social statuses, it was unlikely that Ben would ever love her again, and Phoebe warned herself not to dream impossible dreams. That way lay a broken heart.

For the present, it was enough to be sitting beside the man she loved. Enough to feel the warmth of his powerful body next to hers. Enough to know that she need not think of leaving him until the snow melted sufficiently for her to return to Coalport.

Ben had not spoken for several minutes, apparently lost in thought, but Phoebe was content to ride in silence, just she and her beloved, sleighing through the undisturbed whiteness. The sun sparkled off the snow, making it glint here and there like diamonds dropped by some careless India nabob, and tree branches dipped low, weighed down by melting icicles.

The horse, apparently as happy as Phoebe and Ben to be out in the fresh air, trotted past a copse of evergreen trees, then a small wood filled with larches and Norway maples. Though these were familiar sights to Phoebe, it was only when she noticed the steep-sided banks rising to their left, that it finally occurred to her they would soon be at Iron Bridge.

Too late she realized that if they reached the bridge without mishap, there would be nothing to prevent Ben from driving the sleigh across the massive iron structure and delivering her to Mrs. Curdy's that very day. Suddenly aware that it would break her heart to leave Ben, Phoebe drew breath to bid him turn the gray around that very moment. Before she could speak, however, she heard men's voices in the distance—voices and the unmistakable rhythm of saws being pulled back and forth across wood.

Ben heard them, too, and as the horse rounded the final bend before reaching the bridge, Ben reined in the animal. "Whoa," he called, stopping the gray not far from an uprooted tree.

A stout old larch, easily one-hundred-feet tall, had fallen across the lane just where it met the impressive arched bridge, and on the far side of the tree, six laborers, working two men to a saw, removed the branches then piled them on the bridge. The branches would be taken across to the village, to be used for firewood, and later a team of strong shire horses would pull the body of the tree to the mill where it would be converted into lumber. As yet, the men had not even begun to work on the thick tree trunk or the monstrous roots that reached fifty feet in every direction.

One of the laborers paused long enough to yell to Ben. "The bridge b'aint crossable, gov'ner. Best come back in a few hours. Should be open ter foot traffic by then."

Ben thanked the man and was about to turn the horse and sleigh around when another workman yelled to him. "Yer pardon, sir, but be that young lady Miss Lowell, as lives at Mrs. Curdy's?"

"I am Miss Lowell," Phoebe replied.

The workman touched his forefinger to the bill of his woolen cap. "I'm that pleased ter see ye safe and sound, miss. When the snowstorm come and ye didn't return from yer walk, Mrs. Curdy worrit herself sommit fierce. So happens a search party be planning ter go out ter Wenlock Gorge later today ter look for ye. Only waiting for this 'ere tree ter be got out of the way."

Ben passed the gray's reins to Phoebe, then leapt to the ground and walked over to the tree, motioning for the man who had mentioned Mrs. Curdy to come as close as possible. They spoke for a minute or two, then Ben flipped a coin across the tree. The man caught it in midair. After touching his hat respectfully, he returned to his partner, and soon the two were plying their saw once again, pushing and pulling in a no-nonsense rhythm.

Though filled with curiosity, Phoebe held her tongue, waiting until Ben had resumed his seat and turned the horse around before she asked him what he had said to the laborer.

"I told him who I was," he replied. "Then I gave him some messages to deliver. One to Mr. McNeese, my uncle's solicitor, asking him to come to Holden House with all due speed, bringing with him the constable, the beadle, or the justice of the peace, whoever is responsible for apprehending those who break the law. The other message was for Mrs. Curdy."

"M . . . Mrs. Curdy?"

"I asked the workman to tell your landlady that my great-aunt expects you to dine with her this evening. As well, he is to inform Mrs. Curdy that she need have no further fear for your safety, for I have promised Aunt Constance that I will drive you back to the village some time tomorrow afternoon."

"Thank you. That . . . that was most considerate of you."

They both knew the consideration was not for Mrs. Curdy's nerves, but for Phoebe's reputation. If Ben had said nothing, by nightfall it would have been all over Coalport that the missing china painter was alive, and that she had been seen with an unidentified gentleman.

Now, although the gossip would travel with equal speed through the village, Ben had let it be known that Phoebe was Miss Constance Holden's guest. Such chaperonage was unexceptionable, and as a result of Ben's thoughtfulness, Phoebe could return to her room and to her job with her good name intact.

Though she was grateful for Ben's intervention on her behalf, what pleased Phoebe most was the knowledge that she would not be obliged to return to the village until tomorrow. She would have a few more hours at Holden House, including a full evening spent in the company of the man she loved.

One more evening alone with Ben.

In all likelihood, this would be their last opportunity to share any private time together, and Phoebe was already preparing to store up the memories—memories that would have to last her for a lifetime. Brushing aside thoughts of the future, and the loneliness it might hold, she gave herself up to the joyful prospect of this evening. She had tonight with Ben, and she meant to make the most of it.

One more evening! Ben mulled the words over in his head. After tonight, he might never again have Phoebe all to himself, might never again find a setting that guaranteed him the privacy and seclusion to carry out his plan of seduction. Tonight would be his last opportunity to have his revenge upon her for breaking his heart eight years ago.

He had only this one last evening, and by Heaven, he meant to make the most of it!

Chapter Twelve

"What would I do if I had three wishes? An interesting question, ma'am. Let me think."

"Take your time, my dear."

Miss Constance had enjoyed a good nap, then risen and dressed, complete with powder and patch, and while in Phoebe's company she had enjoyed her tea, consuming a tiny sandwich, two lightly browned seed cakes, and a reviving cup of Bohea. Once she had finished her simple repast, the lady had declared herself feeling more the thing. She had also expressed her happiness at having seen Jamie Whitcombe's ghost, adding that it was actually a relief to know that she need wait no longer for her fiancé's return.

To change the subject, she had asked Phoebe what she would like to have if she were granted three wishes. While the elderly lady drank a second cup of tea, Phoebe considered the question.

"What shall it be, my dear? Adventure? Wealth? Love?"

Phoebe chuckled. "Certainly not adventure, for I have had enough of that in the past few days to last me for a good long time. As for wealth, that has never been one of my ambitions." Phoebe chose not to comment on the third option. She would not speak of love. Some things were far too personal to be offered up for trivial discussion.

"Actually," she continued, "my wants are rather ordinary. First, I would wish that I did not need to return to the village for a few days yet. Then," she added, taking the elderly lady's hand between her own, "I would wish that you might change you mind and agree to join your nephew and me for dinner."

"You are very kind, my dear, but like you, I have had enough excitement for a time. I believe I would be wise to make an early night of it."

Phoebe did not try to persuade the elderly lady to reconsider. Nor did she attempt to dissuade her from sitting beside the window that night, waiting for another glimpse of the "ghost," an occupation she was certain Miss Constance had in mind.

Instead, Phoebe returned to the less serious subject of the third wish. "Finally," she said, looking at the skirt of her dress, then wrinkling her nose in distaste, "I would wish that I did not have to wear this wretched blue merino down to dinner."

After several days of constant and rather harsh usage, the once pretty material was ruined. In addition to being hopelessly wrinkled, the dress exhibited water stains along the hem, the result of melting snow, and the stitching at the left sleeve had broken loose in two places. Trudy had offered to mend the sleeve, then brush and iron the dress, but Phoebe had declined the offer, embarrassed because she had no money with her and would be unable to leave the young maid a suitable vail for the services she had already performed.

Besides, the dress was serviceable at best, and even if it could be made presentable, Phoebe doubted she would set any gentleman's heart afire. "As for these boots," she added, lifting her skirt to exhibit the mudstained leather, "the less said about them the better."

Miss Constance made no reply, merely held her much smaller foot close to Phoebe's, as if comparing their respective sizes. "I cannot lend you any boots," she said, "but I have some slippers that might do the trick."

"But, ma'am, you already gave me some slippers, and they—"

"Pshaw. I do not refer to woolen bed slippers. The ones I have in mind are very special. One might even say they are exotic."

Phoebe tried to decline the offer, fearful of what an elderly lady who still wore an elaborate wig, plus rouge, powder, and patch, might consider exotic. "No, really, ma'am. I was in jest. My boots are fine."

Miss Constance overrode her protests. "Nonsense, my dear. These slippers were made to match a costume I wore to the last party given by my father. Egyptian masquerades were all the rage at that time, and since it was also my eighteenth birthday, Father had my costume made by the most fashionable modiste in London."

Rising, she added, "I could never abide the smell of camphor, so after the ball, when my maid packed the costume away, I would not let her add any protection against moths. For that reason, there is every possibility that the slippers are no longer whole. If they are intact, however, they should serve the purpose."

Since this was the most animated Phoebe had seen Miss Constance that day, she did not bother to inform the lady that slippers—be they ever so well preserved—would be insufficient to transform her. Instead, she held her peace, merely watching while Miss Constance crossed to the far end of the long room, where she stopped before a seaman's chest bound in intricately tooled leather.

It said much for the lady's state of mind that she brushed aside the stacks of daintily sewn shifts and night rails that covered the top of the chest, paying little attention to what befell her sixty-year collection of bride clothes. After lifting the heavy lid, she eased herself down onto her knees and rummaged all the way to the bottom of the chest.

"Aha!" she yelled triumphantly. Having found the items for which she searched, she held them up in full view. "Here they are, my dear. And in perfect condition! What good fortune, to be sure."

"To be sure," Phoebe echoed, albeit with somewhat less enthusiasm. She schooled her face to hide her initial reaction, for the things Miss Constance held aloft so proudly—Phoebe disdained to call them footwear—were the most peculiar-looking items she had ever seen. Fashioned of dark gold velvet, they were trimmed across the instep in black braid, and the toes, other than being pointed, were almost comically elongated, more like elves' shoes than anything an Egyptian might wear.

"Come, my dear. See if they will fit."

Having let the hunt go this far, Phoebe could not now decline the offer, so she kept her feelings to herself. After unlacing and removing her boots, she padded across the carpeted floor to the chest, all the while saying a silent prayer that the slippers would not fit her much larger feet.

To her dismay, the first one slipped on as though it had been made especially for her. When the second one slipped on with equal ease, Phoebe was obliged to swallow any further excuses. Knowing she would never wear them, yet unwilling to hurt Miss Constance's feelings, Phoebe smiled and thanked her for her kindness. "I shall take very good care of them, ma'am, and return them to you in the morning."

Before Phoebe could reclaim her boots and make good her escape, the elderly lady bid her wait, then began rummaging once again in the chest. "What luck, my dear. You will not have to wear your blue merino after all, for I have found the costume as well."

For just a moment, Phoebe's heart stood still. She was almost afraid to see for herself what sort of costume suited the very peculiar slippers. When she looked up from lacing her boots, however, and saw the dress draped across Miss Constance's arm, her breath caught in her throat. The costume was nothing like the panniered monstrosity Phoebe had expected. Far from it!

Though not at all certain what Egyptian ladies wore more than half a century ago, Phoebe doubted it was anything like the pale green silk Miss Constance brought forward and laid across Phoebe's lap. Judging by the soft draping of the delicate fabric, the style was more representative of the fashions of early Greece.

"Oh, my," she breathed, running her fingertips along the filmy folds. "It is exquisite. But . . . but I cannot possibly wear it. The silk is much too fine, and I should be frightened every minute that I might spill something."

Miss Constance ignored her entirely. "There is a shawl," she said, returning to the chest and unearthing a length of silk woven with alternating gold and green stripes. "You will need this, for the top of the costume was rather revealing, even by the standards of my day."

"But—"

"Oh, and this is the piece I wound around my head to form the turban. Of course, you will need the clips that hold the material in place." The second length of silk was striped like the shawl, and the two gold-colored clips, which had reposed in a little velvet drawstring bag, were shaped like some exotic bird.

When the clips were dropped into Phoebe's hand, she was surprised to discover that the birds were not painted, as she had thought, but were made of actual gold, their eyes represented by real diamonds. Though unable to credit that such valuable jewelry had lain in a chest, forgotten for so many years, she kept her remarks to herself, passing the clips back to their owner. "The birds are beautiful, ma'am, but under no circumstances would I borrow them."

"But, my dear, the clips are a part of the ensemble. As for the costume, the style makes it easy to fit, and once you tie the gold cord around your waist, you will find it a simple matter to adjust the length of the skirt to suit your added height. As for the color, the pale green is perfect for your eyes."

Phoebe made several further attempts to convince the elderly lady that she could not possibly wear such a costume; unfortunately, all her arguments fell on unlistening ears. In time, she decided the easiest course of action would be to thank Miss Constance, then take everything to her bedchamber as though she meant to wear it. Since the lady would not be joining them for dinner, she need never know that Phoebe had not worn the finery.

While Phoebe was being presented with the not-so-Egyptian costume, Ben took the horse and sleigh for another ride, this time in the opposite direction from Iron Bridge. Deciding to see how close he could get to Shrewsbury, he was more than happy to meet an ancient gig coming from that direction, traveling toward him at a slow, careful pace. His disposition improved even more when the driver of the dun-colored animal drew close enough for Ben to recognize the man's carrot-red hair.

"Fortson! It seems we were of like minds, for I had hoped I might find you."

Edgar Fortson reined in the rawboned horse, cursing beneath his breath when the animal continued for several more steps before coming to a complete stop. "My lord," the valet greeted him, "I'm that glad to meet ye, sir, for I'd no notion how far I might get in this snow, nor how long I might depend upon this bag of bad points."

Knowing how the Scotsman prided himself on his handling of the ribbons, Ben smiled at the disreputable horse. "May I assume, since you are tooling a less than elegant equipage, that my coach and driver returned to town, with both passengers inside?"

"As ye instructed, sir. I saw them off myself this very morning, soon as the sun came out and began to melt a bit of the snow. Once they were on their way, I hired this four-legged creature—I refuse to call him a horse—and set out for Holden House. On account of I heard something I felt ye would want to know right away."

Ben was not surprised that his wiry little batman-turned-valet had learned something of interest. Fortson was only five-foot-three, and he weighed less than eight stone soaking wet, and for that reason people were apt to pour all manner of gossip into his ear, thinking his lack of stature rendered him harmless. Actually, nothing could be further from the truth, for as Ben had discovered during their years together in the Peninsula, there was no handier man to have around in times of trouble than Edgar Fortson.

"While in the taproom at the Tawny Lion," the valet began, "I bought a pint for a fellow down on his luck, just being friendly like, and discovered that up until six months ago he had been the coachman-groom at Holden House."

"The devil, you say!"

"Right, sir. Seems this fellow had worked for the previous Lord Holden for more than twenty years, or so he said. Then after the old lord went to his maker, suddenly the groom was let go. For no reason. Him and several other servants. Nobody left at the house, he claims, 'cept for an old cowherd and the housekeeper and her husband. The husband, Abbott's his name, is a havey-cavey sort of idler who was used to work in the taproom of a right seedy public house on the far side of Shrewsbury."

"Havey-cavey, eh? That certainly describes Henry Abbott. An idler with a thirst. As for his working in the taproom, I would not be surprised to learn that my new butler was let go from his previous employment for drinking up all the profits."

"That's as may be, sir, but the fellow as was groom said that Abbott had stumbled into the taproom of the Tawny Lion not more than a week ago. He'd been drinking heavy like, before he got there, and when none of the local men would stand him a pint, he started bragging about how he was coming into a large sum of money in the very near future. Enough money, so he boasted, to buy his own public house, at which none of the stingy-guts present would be welcome."

"Charming fellow," Ben said, "with a decided knack for making friends. But do go on, Fortson, you see me hanging on your every word."

The valet hid his smile. "I thought ye'd be interested, sir. 'Specially when ye hear the rest of the story."

"The rest?"

"Yes, sir. Seems this Abbott was so jug-bitten he couldn't keep his mummer shut. Told more than he should have." The valet paused for just a moment. "Begging your pardon for this next part, my lord, but Abbott claimed the Holdens were all queer in their attics, a fact that made his job so easy it was like taking a sweet from a wee bairn."

Ben ignored the slur on his family. After all, Abbott was no Sir Isaac Newton. Ben could not have cared less about the opinion of some drunken sot; what he wanted to hear was what the lout was up to. "By his 'job' I take it my devoted employee did not mean his duties as butler."

"No, sir. According to the groom, Abbott continued by saying that all he had to do to get his future pile of money was to see the job was done before the new Lord Holden took up residence."

Ben was quiet for a time, as though lost in thought. Finally, he said, "Did Abbott mention what that job might be?"

"He didn't get the opportunity, sir. Seems another fellow came into the taproom, and obviously he'd been searching all over Shrewsbury for Abbott. A different sort of fellow this one was. Younger, slimmer, and sober as a magistrate, plus he looked angry enough to bite the head off a frog. The newcomer arrived just in time to overhear the last part of Abbott's conversation, and without a word he crossed the taproom and planted Abbott a facer, knocking him to the ground. Right handy with his fives, the new fellow was."

Ben had known something was going on at Holden House, he just had not been able to discover what was afoot. Now, Fortson had supplied a few of the missing pieces to the puzzle. "I wonder," Ben said, "did you happen to discover the name of the man who knocked Abbott down?"

The valet nodded. "Name's Whitcombe, sir. Jamie Whitcombe."

Chapter Thirteen

"Counting Abbott," Ben said, "there are three of them. At least that is my suspicion. One of the malefactors was seen by my aunt's guest, and you will understand my instant dislike of the fellow when I tell you he manhandled Miss Lowell, forcing her to defend herself from his unwanted advances."

"The villain! Was the lady injured?"

"Only frightened, but you can understand my wish to lay hands on the fellow myself. There is a score to be settled."

"Right, sir. Can't let a lady be manhandled without . . ." He blinked. "Your pardon, mylord, but did ye say, Miss Lowell?"

Ben swore. He had forgotten Fortson's uncanny recall of names and faces. "Never mind," he said, "for the lady will be leaving on the morrow. Our most pressing concern is those rascals holed up in the stables. With the way clear to Shrewsbury, I suspect they will make their move sometime this evening, then be gone as fast as possible."

"We'll see can we slow them down a bit," Fortson said. "Be my pleasure, sir, to take part in their coming disappointment."

"Good man. Here is my plan. If you have anything to add, pray, do not stand on ceremony."

The two men concluded their business while still some way from the estate, away from prying eyes and listening ears. After Fortson confirmed that he did, indeed, have his holster pistol, the valet took up the ribbons again and followed the sleigh to within half a mile of Holden House.

To allow his employer time to get to the house without anyone suspecting they had been together, making plans, Fortson waited in the lane, out of sight, for a full twenty minutes, then he drove the gig onto the carriageway and around to the kitchen entrance. Once he had handed the hired horse over to Abbott, who declared himself more than willing to take the animal to the stable, Fortson carried his employer's traps up to the master bedchamber and busied himself with putting the new Lord Holden's clothes away.

"Happen this linen needs ironing," he said sometime later, taking a perfectly crisp cravat and wadding it into a ball. "I'd be remiss in putting it away all crumpled like, so with your permission, sir, I'll go belowstairs to see if this ramshackle establishment boasts anything resembling a mangle."

Waiting only for Ben's nod of approval, Fortson opened the bedchamber door slightly before he continued. "Since I'll be in the kitchen anyway, I believe I'll linger long enough to have me a bite to eat and wet my whistle with a bit of home brew." Lowering his voice, he said, "While I'm at it, I'll see what I can learn from the housekeeper and her husband."

With a wink, he added more loudly, "By your leave, my lord, I'll have Abbott put that sorry bag of bones to the hired gig, so's I can return the conveyance to Shrewsbury."

Ben winked in return. "Do what you must," he replied, adding a touch of boredom to his voice for good measure.

"Thank you, sir. Wouldn't want to have to pay another full day's rate for the hire. Half a quid, that bandit at the Tawny Lion charged me for the gig and that sorry excuse for a horse. I'll be the richer for it if I return them now, remain at the inn for the night, then give one of the ostlers a shilling to bring me back in the morning."

"Have the housekeeper show you where you may put your traps," Ben said. "But be warned, Fortson. No matter the weather, I will expect you back here first thing tomorrow morning. Without fail."

"Tomorrow it is. You may rely on me, my lord. I'll leave the inn at first light, so I can be back here before you're ready to break your fast."

After taking tea with Miss Constance, Phoebe had returned to her silver-and-lilac bedchamber, removed her dress and boots, then lain down on her narrow bed for a short rest. Unfortunately, the intended rest had turned into sound sleep, and she might have remained there into the night had she not heard an unfamiliar voice in the corridor.

"*Tomorrow it is*," someone had said rather loudly. Then they had mentioned something about breaking a fast. After that there had been the sound of footfalls going in the direction of the servants' stairs.

At first, unable to identify the voice, Phoebe had felt a frisson of fear, but by the time she had tiptoed to the door to assure herself that all was well, whoever had awakened her was out of sight.

Not that it mattered. Phoebe was happy someone had awakened her, for if she had slept through her last evening at Holden House, she would have been heartbroken. In fact, she had planned to go belowstairs even before time for dinner, so she would not miss so much as a minute in Ben's company.

With time of the essence, she hurried across the bare floor to the oak washstand, stripped off her shift and drawers, then poured tepid water into the earthenware bowl and washed herself from head to foot.

Once she had donned the last of the fresh underthings Miss Constance had given her, Phoebe combed out her hair, taking extra time to arrange it in a becoming knot atop her head—a knot from which little tendrils spilled across her temples and against the nape of her neck.

The nap had done her a world of good, and she admitted, if only to herself, that she was in good looks. "What a shame I must ruin the effect by stepping into my soiled blue merino."

She had only just uttered the words, then turned to retrieve the pale blue wool from the wall peg where she had hung it earlier, when she received a surprise. The dress was gone! Her cloak was missing as well, leaving her nothing to cover herself with—nothing save the pale green Egyptian costume Miss Constance had taken from the seaman's chest.

The costume, complete with shawl and turban, hung on the wall pegs where once the wool dress and cloak had been, and the gold slippers sat on the floor just beneath the ensemble. All three silk pieces had been pressed with such care that the delicate material looked freshly spun, instead of decades' old. Lastly, one of the diamond-eyed gold birds had been used to pin a note to the bodice of the dress.

> *My dear girl,*
> *The merino will be returned to your room later this evening. In the meantime, please wear the Egyptian costume. You will look beautiful in it, and it will make me happy knowing that you got at least one of your three wishes.*
>
> *Your friend,*
> *Constance Holden*

Ben had ordered a special dinner for his and Phoebe's last evening together, and before Fortson left, the ever-resourceful valet had unearthed a bottle of French champagne from the previous Lord Holden's nearly empty wine cellar.

With seduction in mind, Ben had taken special pains with his appearance, happy to be able to ignore his uncle's outdated wardrobe and the deceased's poorly stropped razor. Ben had employed his own specially forged blade to ensure a close shave, then he had donned his newest evening attire, the claret-colored coat and pantaloons he had received from Weston only a few days before leaving London. The coat was worn over a cream-colored waistcoat, while a modest, yet costly, black pearl stud reposed in the folds of his perfectly tied cravat.

He had hoped to impress Phoebe with his sartorial splendor, but the moment he entered the candlelit library and beheld the object of his planned seduction, he forgot everything save the woman who literally took his breath away and all but turned him to stone.

Somewhere in the back of his mind, Ben recalled thinking that Phoebe was no longer as beautiful as she had been eight years ago. He must remember to get his eyes examined when next he was in London, for the woman who stood before the fireplace, waiting for him, was without doubt the most beautiful creature he had ever seen.

She wore some sort of flowing gown whose skirt only just covered her shins. Not content with leaving her slender ankles exposed, the skirt clung to her rounded hips and her long legs in a manner that made Ben's blood grow warm in his veins. He might have thought Phoebe had dampened her petticoats had it not been for the fact that she wore none—a circumstance revealed all too clearly by the firelight that burned brightly behind her.

The gown was vaguely Grecian looking, with the gathered silk of the bodice criss-crossing over her lovely breasts, then tying atop each shoulder. A surprising amount of her bosom was exposed, even though she had draped a transparent shawl across her chest, then tucked the gold-and-green striped silk beneath the tied shoulders, allowing the remainder of the material to flow down her back.

Her slender waist was circled by a golden cord, and on her feet were the most outlandish-looking slippers Ben had ever seen. And yet, the pointed-toed footwear suited both the lady and her costume.

She had done something different and altogether charming with her hair, and using a pair of gold pins, she had clipped the ends of a second, shorter length of striped silk on each side of her head, allowing the transparent material to fall in loose folds across the lower potion of her face.

The veil-like effect was so exotic, so mesmerizing, that Ben could not find words to express his enchantment. While he stared, Phoebe placed her palms together just in front of her face, then she inclined her head in a bow worthy of an Eastern princess. "Good evening, my lord. My name is Scheherazade, and I await your pleasure."

If Ben had been speechless before, that artless little greeting left him bereft of both thought and movement. Still unable to credit the vision before his eyes, he merely stood in the center of the room and looked his fill of Phoebe's beautiful face and figure. Her soft chuckle finally broke the spell that held him immobile, and he was able to continue toward the fireplace.

"Fair princess," he said, lifting her hand to his lips, "you take me quite by surprise."

Phoebe's smile was only faintly visible behind the silk veil, and Ben was tempted to kiss his way up the satiny skin of her bare arm, his destination her alluring mouth.

"I am a bit surprised myself," she said. "Though I

told Miss Constance I could not wear the costume, once I had donned it, I own I began to get into the spirit of the thing."

"Remind me," he said, leading Phoebe toward the settee, "to send my aunt a note expressing my gratitude for the gift."

"Oh, it was not a gift. I merely borrowed it."

"The gift," he said softly, "was to me."

Phoebe's cheeks grew warm with pleasure. Her looking glass had told her that she looked especially nice this evening, but it was wonderful to know that Ben thought her attractive. She was still tingling from the compliment when Abbott arrived, bearing a large silver tray on which reposed two plates, complete with pewter warming domes, and a pair of crystal wineglasses.

To her surprise, the butler was sober, clean shaven, and surprisingly alert. And if he was not dressed in attire appropriate to his position in a gentleman's establishment, at least his coat was pressed and his shirt and cravat were clean, almost making her forget about the cuts and bruises on his face.

By not so much as a raised eyebrow did he acknowledge Phoebe's unusual raiment; it was almost as if the veiled costume did not register in his brain. Furthermore, there was something in the butler's eyes she had never seen before—a brightness that could not be hidden.

"Dinner, my lord." When Abbott spoke those three words, his mouth very nearly broke into a smile, and if Phoebe had not known it to be impossible, she would have thought the servant had just received word that he had come into a fortune. What else could account for the enthusiasm in his manner and expression?

He set the tray on the small occasional table they

had used earlier that day. Then he bowed politely and excused himself to fetch the wine.

"My word," she said once the library door was shut, "one must wonder what has wrought this unexpected transformation in Abbott's manner. He appears positively imbued with vigor. And though I am persuaded he is sober, he seems almost drunk with excitement. Dare we hope that his improved outlook will last through the entire evening? Or even through tomorrow?"

"I believe," Ben replied slowly, "that his excitement will last throughout *this* evening, for unless I miss my guess, the fellow has plans for later tonight. As for tomorrow, who can tell what tomorrow may bring?"

He said no more, but if the sudden darkening of his eyes was anything to go by, Ben knew something—something he had not told Phoebe. Something he did not intend to tell her. Not that she wanted to be included in the secret. She hoped tomorrow would bring the constable and a posse of armed men to Holden House. For now, however, Phoebe had only these final few hours with the man she loved, and she did not wish to spend them discussing whatever nefarious plot Abbott and his "ghostly" accomplice were up to.

The door opened again and Abbott returned with a mahogany cellaret containing a bottle of champagne wrapped in a linen napkin. After setting the cellaret on the floor beside the occasional table, he asked, most politely, "Shall I open the wine, my lord?"

"Yes," Ben replied. "Then you may seek your bed if that is your choice. I have no further need of you this evening, and under no circumstances do I wish to be disturbed."

"Yes, my lord. I'll see don't nobody disturb you."

Phoebe had never seen the face of a fox planning to visit the poultry house, but she could not believe the expression on the fox's face would differ noticeably from the look presently occupying Henry Abbott's battered visage. The servant all but laughed aloud at Ben's orders, and after bowing politely once again, he quit the library at a less-than-leisurely pace.

Unable to keep silent, she said, "Ben, that man is up to something."

"I quite agree, but let us not ruin our evening by talking about Abbott." He smiled to smooth over any unintentional harshness in his tone. "What say you we make a pact?"

"A pact?"

"Yes. To discuss nothing and no one but us. Just you and me."

The words were sweet music to Phoebe's ears. "Just you and me," she repeated.

"Then let us seal the bargain with a glass of champagne." Ben filled the glasses with the sparkling wine, then he touched his glass to hers, the delicate crystal pinging like a tiny bell.

"To you," Phoebe said.

"To you as well, Scheherazade, and to our last evening together. May it be a memorable one for us both."

At his softly spoken words, Phoebe felt warmth travel up her spine—a warmth that seemed to find its way to her midsection, where it started a small fire. In hopes of putting out that flame before it consumed her, she pushed aside her veil and drank the entire contents of the glass. Ben drank his glass empty as well, but if the bubbly liquid was required to extinguish a flame inside him, he kept the fact to himself.

After returning the crystal to the tray, he lifted the pewter warming covers; then, with an exaggerated bow, he declared himself her servant for the evening. "Allow me," he said, making a great show of spreading a large linen napkin across her lap. While Phoebe stifled a giggle, he handing her an ornately carved silver fork and one of the plates, already served with escallops of veal and small green peas with tiny onions.

Taking the second plate for himself, he did not sit in the wing chair, as she expected, but made himself comfortable on the polar bear rug, stretching his long, elegantly clad legs out toward the hearth. He looked totally relaxed, and Phoebe wished he had invited her to join him on the thick white fur.

"Veal," she said, hoping to take her mind off her disappointment at not being able to sit closer to Ben. "Is it still your favorite?"

"It is," he said, smiling up at her in a way that positively melted her heart. "Escalloped veal, a bottle of wine, and a fascinating companion with whom to enjoy them. A man could ask for nothing more."

Nor could a woman!

While Ben speared one of the small cubes of meat with his fork, then lifted the food to his mouth, a single thought echoed inside Phoebe's brain. *Lucky veal!*

While he licked his lips in enjoyment of the food, she reached up to remove the veil so she could eat as well. Holding her plate with one hand, she raised the other to one of the diamond-eyed birds; then, after pulling the clip free, she let the silk fall to her right shoulder.

It was an innocent act, not intended to seduce, but when Phoebe removed the veil, Ben very nearly choked on the food that suddenly seemed far too large to swallow. Damnation! What was wrong with him? He had seen women by the dozens disrobe completely, and being a normal male he had always enjoyed the sight. But he had never witnessed anything so heart-stopping as Phoebe removing that one piece of cloth. The blood positively pounded in his head, and he wanted nothing so much as to toss his dinner—plate and all—into the fire and pull Phoebe down onto the bearskin rug beside him, where he could kiss her until she begged for more.

Careful, old boy. Seduction requires finesse, not cave-man tactics. Thinking it wise to give his thoughts a new direction, he asked Phoebe if he might pour her another glass of champagne.

She shook her head. "I know you do not remember the night we met, Ben, but you just repeated the first words you ever spoke to me."

This time, Ben honestly did not remember the incident. "A rather unusual first remark, surely."

"Not so very odd, considering the fact that while Lady Carrington introduced us, I held a glass of champagne in my hand. My uncle and I were guests at the come-out ball given for her ladyship's niece, Sophia, and though the night was already half gone, *you* had only just arrived."

Putting Ben in mind of the storyteller in the Arabian tale, Phoebe set her plate back on the tray and folded her hands in her lap, giving her full attention to her reminiscences. "Sophia Carrington and I were enjoying our first Season, and at that particular moment, *I* was also enjoying my very first glass of champagne."

"Then I showed up, fashionably late."

"Unforgivably late," she countered, making him chuckle.

"Like many a young man, I had not yet learned that the world does not revolve around me. Was I insufferably conceited?"

"Not at all. In fact, you wore your Regimentals, and I thought you the handsomest man I had ever seen."

Ben uttered a sound of disgust. "Why, I wonder, does the image of a strutting peacock come to mind?"

"No, no! You were splendid, I assure you. In fact, you broke the heart of every female at the ball. Me included. As well, you exhibited such polish, and seemed so debonair, that I felt unbelievably nervous in your company."

"Miss Phoebe Lowell, nervous? Now that, I will not believe."

"Oh, it is true. When you did not simply acknowledge the introduction and move on to some other, more sophisticated lady, my mouth went dry as toast, rendering me incapable of speech. To relieve the situation, I drank the entire glass of champagne in two long gulps."

"At which time, I delivered my memorable line about pouring you another glass."

"Actually, you asked if you might *procure* another glass of champagne for me, and though my uncle had warned me that I must stop at the one, I nodded my permission. Quick as a wink, you captured two glasses from the tray of a passing footman, the move so smoothly executed that you did not spill so much as a drop of the wine."

Ben laughed aloud. "What a damned coxcomb I was! That particular move was smooth because I had practiced it countless times before a looking glass in the privacy of my rooms. I am ashamed to admit that I employed the trick at every party, expressly to impress upon the ladies what a fine fellow I was!"

The moment the words left his lips, Ben realized his mistake. Forgetting about his supposed amnesia, he had admitted to remembering something from his past. Fortunately, Phoebe appeared not to notice the slip. She merely laughed, then resumed her story.

"Your tactic worked, sir, for I was vastly impressed, yet still so nervous I could think of nothing intelligent to say. While you sipped at your wine, as any sensible person would, I made short work of mine once again. Needless to say, by the time you suggested we have something to eat, I had developed a full-blown case of the hiccups."

She sighed. "I wanted you to think me quite grown up, and there I was hiccupping like a schoolroom chit, the sound so loud I did not doubt it could be heard from John O'Groats to Land's End. Everyone in the room was laughing at me."

Now Ben remembered. There were dozens of couples partaking of the refreshments in Lady Carrington's dining room, and each time Phoebe hiccupped, someone new joined in the laughter. Phoebe had laughed as well, revealing those adorable dimples, and Ben had been hard-pressed not to lean down and kiss her smiling mouth.

By the third hiccup, he was a goner! He had looked into those lovely gray-green eyes, and every other lady in the room disappeared.

While Phoebe continued her story, Ben concentrated on her face. The dimples were not so pronounced now, but the eyes were as lovely as ever, and at the moment the light from the fire was turning those orbs the same pale green as the silk of her costume.

The firelight was also lending a golden glow to her satiny skin, and just looking at her bare arms and shoulders was tightening Ben's cravat to a dangerous degree. Heaven help him! He did not think he could wait much longer to begin the planned seduction, for every nerve in his body cried out for him to take Phoebe in his arms and plunder the sweet depths of her mouth.

"By the way," he said, his voice not as steady as he would have liked, "did I forget to tell you how lovely you look this evening?"

"Yes. I mean, no." She blushed prettily. "What I should say is, you did not mention it."

When her tongue flicked out to moisten her bottom lip, Ben watched in fascination, quite certain he could hear the blood surging through his veins. In fact, he marveled that Phoebe did not question the sudden noise.

He tried to school his visage not to reveal what was going on inside him. Unfortunately, his feelings must have shown on his face, for Phoebe blushed again, then she stood and walked over to the walnut knee-hole desk, on the pretext of adjusting one of the candles in the candelabra. After straightening the guttering candle, she rested her hands on the ladder-back chair to keep them still.

If Ben had not seen the way her hands trembled, and realized that she was as excited as he by the undeniable attraction between them, he might have remained beside the fireplace. As it was, he could not cross the room fast enough.

He stopped just behind her. "Please," he said softly, "do not feel you must run from me, my beautiful one."

Phoebe's breath caught in her throat. Before this moment, no one had ever called her beautiful—not even her parents—and if she lived to be a hundred years old, she would never forget that it was Ben Holden who had said it to her.

He was behind her, standing so close that she fancied she could feel the warmth of his skin heating hers. She dared not turn around, for if he saw her face, he might realize how much she wanted him to take her in his arms . . . how much she longed to have him hold her close and kiss her.

"Pretty Phoebe," he said, the words so soft she wondered if she had only imagined them, "please come back to the fire."

He put his hands on her bare shoulders, and the instant he touched her, she knew she would return with him to the fire, or die trying.

His strong fingers began to move slowly against her skin, and at his mesmerizing touch, her entire body began to tremble. She thought he might turn her to face him, but he merely eased his hands down her arms, not stopping until he reached her wrists. For a moment, his thumbs teased the sensitive area on the inside of her wrists, then he captured her right hand and entwined his fingers with hers.

"Come," he said, gently leading her back to the hearth.

Though her heart beat like some primitive drum inside her chest, it never occurred to Phoebe to say him nay. She was so nervous her knees very nearly refused to sustain her for the short walk, yet never once did it cross her mind to tell him to unhand her.

She knew Ben's purpose in taking her back to the hearth, and it was *not* so she could finish her dinner. She was certain that food was the last thing on his mind, just as it was the last thing on hers.

"Come," he said again, and this time when he sat on the soft, white fur of the polar bear rug, he urged Phoebe to join him. Not that she needed any coaxing. Ben Holden was the man she loved, and whatever he wanted her to do, that was the very thing she wanted.

Chapter Fourteen

For a time they merely sat quietly and watched the mingled blue and yellow flames of the fire, their shoulders touching. Phoebe was beginning to think she had misinterpreted the situation, and that Ben did not feel the same magical pull toward her as she felt toward him, when he slowly bent his head and pressed his mouth to the side of her neck.

She breathed in sharply, not from surprise at his kiss, but from the overwhelming need she felt to have those lips on hers. Phoebe was twenty-seven-years old, a spinster by anyone's reckoning, and during the past eight years, no one had even hugged her. Now, here she sat beside the man she loved, with him kissing her, and she could not believe that it was *her* feeling such passion, or that she was willing to give Ben her love without any pledge from him in return.

She barely recognized herself. Was this the same Phoebe Lowell who had once refused Ben's marriage proposal because he either could not or would not give her the assurance she needed that he would love her forever, and never leave her?

This time she asked for no such assurances. She knew better. This evening might well be all she would ever have of Ben Holden, and she meant to enjoy it. She wanted this moment. She needed it. Whatever happened between them, these were the memories she would take back to Coalport with her. These were

he memories she would keep inside her heart for all
he years of her life.

Emboldened by her need, she lay her hand on Ben's
chest, where the steady beat of his heart against her
palm prompted her own heart to speed up its pace to
match his. Unable to stop herself, she looked up into
his dark eyes, no longer caring that she might expose
her vulnerability, or reveal how much she loved him.

She was rewarded for her boldness when he placed
his hand on her shoulder, turning her slightly so he
could brush his lips ever so softly across her brow. His
breath was warm, his lips unbelievably soft, and
though Phoebe could have stayed there forever, never
letting go of that fragile, precious moment, the kiss
was over almost as soon as it began.

"Sweet Phoebe," he breathed against her temple.

"Ben," she replied, her voice sounding oddly husky,
almost pleading.

As if sensing what she wanted, he slipped his hand
around to the nape of her neck. Phoebe closed her
eyes, wanting to savor the sensuous feel of his palm
against her skin. His strong fingers moved upward
into her hair, sending shivers of delight all the way to
her toes, and when his hand cupped the back of her
head, it stole every coherent thought from her brain,
and the last shreds of her pride.

Ben urged her head toward his, and after what
seemed an eternity, their lips touched in a feather-
light kiss. Phoebe treasured those first magical moments, delighting in the clean, male fragrance of him,
but soon she wanted to deepen the contact. Instinctu-
ally, she leaned forward, and was rewarded beyond
her wildest dreams.

His mouth claimed hers, and instantly Phoebe felt a
giant wave of heat engulf her. Both excited and frightened by the force of that heat, her first reaction was to
pull away.

Stay! something inside her shouted. *No retreating.*
No thinking. Just feeling. This was what she had hoped
would happen tonight, and she refused to let some
leftover girlish uncertainty make her cry craven. No!
now.

The kiss continued, and Phoebe was hypnotized by
the heady taste of him . . . by the firm, sure grip of his
hand at her head . . . by the solid strength of his hard-
muscled body so close she could reach out and touch
it. And she wanted to touch him; more than she had
ever wanted anything in her life. She wanted to know
every inch of him; she longed to touch and explore his
body to her heart's content.

As clearly as if some phantom hand had written it
on the wall for her to read, Phoebe suddenly understood those unnamed, restless yearnings that had
plagued her dreams these past few years. It was the
primitive call of her own body, wanting to know how
it felt to be loved by a man.

No! The call might be primitive, but Phoebe was
not. She did not want to be loved by just any man.
She wanted to know how it would feel to have the
man she loved make love to her. She wanted to know
how it felt to be loved by *Ben.*

Phoebe was still reeling from the realization of
what she wanted, when Ben broke the kiss and slowly
removed his hand. Thankfully, he did not move away,
and reassured, Phoebe tried to curb those yearnings
Ben had awakened, telling herself to wait patiently for
him to kiss her again.

She could be patient! She was certain she could.
Even though she had never wanted anything in her
life as badly as she wanted him to touch her again . . .
to claim her mouth again . . . she waited.

Ben drew in a ragged breath. He had never experienced such lust! A few light kisses, and he was already aflame with longing. He could take Phoebe

ow, he knew it to be true, for the truth was there in
er eyes. She wanted him as much as he wanted her.

And yet, he hesitated.

Oddly enough, something stopped him. He could
ot even guess what. He was seducing her, just as he
ad planned, so why was he plagued by this sense of
reboding—this uneasy feeling that by attaining his
oal now, he might forfeit something infinitely pre-
ous?

Was he losing his mind?

All he knew for certain was that before he made
ove to her, before he had his revenge on her for the
eartache she had dealt him eight years ago, he
anted something from her. Something freely given.
le wanted her to put her arms around him and kiss
im without any prompting, without any coercion on
is part.

What foolishness was this? Ben had Phoebe just
here he wanted her, and if he was not careful he
ould lose the upper hand.

Hand! Heaven help him! The very word sent a
pasm of desire though him. He wanted to feel
hoebe's hands explore his chest, his shoulders, his
eck—every inch of him—just as he wanted to ex-
lore every soft, curvaceous inch of her. He longed to
ave her naked body molded against his; just the
ought of it was exquisite torture. As for making love
o her, he positively ached just thinking of it.

In the past eight years, Ben had known many
omen—willing women, women who knew how to
ake a man's blood flame with passion—and yet, he
ad never known such desire as this. He had never
nown such need to be with one woman and one
oman only.

And not just any woman.

Not some nameless, faceless woman. He wanted
hoebe Lowell.

He wanted *Phoebe's* kiss. He wanted *Phoebe's* body close to his. He wanted to feel Phoebe's heart beating wildly beneath his hand . . . to hear her breath grow labored. He wanted to teach her the joys of passion; to show her what love could be between a man and a woman; and to hear her cry out his name.

And afterward, when she was all soft and warm and fulfilled, he wanted to hold her in his arms and hear her whisper words of love in his ear.

Words of love!

The realization of his feelings was almost painful, robbing Ben of breath. The truth hit him hard, like well-placed fists striking blow after blow to his solar plexus, unrelenting and inescapable. And in that moment, Ben knew he wanted to make love to Phoebe, not just this once, but a hundred times. A thousand times. A million times over!

In his entire life, he had never wanted anything so much.

"Ben," Phoebe whispered, "please, kiss me again."

"No," he said, his throat so tight he had trouble getting the word past it.

Despite the negative reply, the hoarseness of Ben's voice sent a thrill through Phoebe, making every inch of her body tingle. She knew he did not mean that he did not *want* to kiss her again.

He looked at her for a long time, his eyes grown darker than the night, and finally he said, "You kiss *me.*"

Phoebe would have preferred that *he* kiss *her*, for he knew better what to do, but she could no more resist his invitation than she could make herself cease to draw breath. Putting aside her fears that he might think her far too gauche, she leaned close to him, pausing when her lips were but a whisper away from his. "Ben, I . . . I do not know how to—"

"You are doing fine," he said, the words so soft Phoebe was not certain she had not imagined them.

Inflamed by the warmth of his breath on her cheek, she moved that final inch and touched her lips to his. The contact was tentative at best, but instantly heat surged throughout her body. When she leaned even closer, allowing her soft breasts to find a home against his hard chest, the heat that had raced through her grew even hotter, turning her bones to liquid fire, before settling in those secret, unexplored regions of her body.

Of their own accord, her lips parted, and as if answering some unspoken invitation of hers, Ben's tongue touched her lips, teasing them, tantalizing them until Phoebe grew lightheaded. When she thought she could not endure the sweet torment a moment longer, his tongue slipped gently between her lips, making her moan.

"My beautiful Scheherazade," Ben whispered against her mouth. Then he gathered her in his strong arms, molding every inch of her willing body to the hard length of his. Finally, he kissed her as she longed to be kissed, and the joy of that kiss threatened to shatter her heart into a thousand pieces.

This, then, was what Phoebe had been waiting for all those years. She had been waiting for Ben. For his arms around her, holding her close. For him loving her as she had always longed to be loved.

He drew her even closer, and somehow she was no longer sitting up, but lying on the rug, the soft, sensuous white fur caressing her bare shoulders. Within moments, the room, the fireplace, the rug itself disappeared; she and Ben were the only two people in the world, and he was moving aside the silk shawl so his lips could rain kisses down her neck and across her exposed chest, his mouth bringing every inch of her skin to life.

"Ben," she whispered, "I love you so much."

"What, sweetings?" He barely heard her, for he wa busy paying homage to the enticing valley betwee the swell of her beautiful breasts.

"I love you," she said. "I never stopped lovin you."

This time Ben heard her. He drew back. It was th most difficult thing he had ever done, but he had t be certain he had not mistaken her words. "What di you say?"

"I have never loved anyone but you," she said. "M heart is, and always has been, yours."

My heart is, and always has been, yours.

Shaken by Phoebe's words, Ben got to his feet, step ping back almost to the hearth. *Did she mean it? Coul it be possible that she had never stopped loving him? Coul he have so misjudged her all these years?*

Riddled with a combination of guilt and uncer tainty, and needing time to think, he walked over t the desk, putting as much distance as possible be tween them. Once his head was cleared, albeit only little, he realized there was but one sane thing to do He must send Phoebe away until he had time t think. Until they both had time to think without th distorting influence of passion.

After removing a single candle from the candelabra he retraced his steps. "Here," he said, offering th candle to Phoebe.

She sat up. Though her lips were still full and rip from his kisses, her eyes were hazy with bewilder ment. "Ben, I—"

"To light your way to your bedchamber," he said offering her the candle once again. He reached dowr his hand to help her to her feet, but she did not take it.

Like one awakened abruptly from a sound sleep she stared first at his outstretched hand, then at him

"I do not understand," she said. "Did I do something wrong?"

"Come," he said, and this time she took his hand and allowed him to help her stand.

Once she was steady on her feet, she looked him directly in the eyes, as if she hoped to find an explanation there for his sudden coldness. "Please, Ben. Was it what I said? Tell me."

Tell her? How could he tell this beautiful, giving woman that he had lied to her from the very beginning, and that he had planned to take her innocence, then toss her aside? And all in the name of revenge. How could he tell her that he was ashamed of himself? Ashamed that he had ever thought he was entitled to hurt her.

What a cruel word: *revenge*. Cruel and mean spirited, and too late Ben realized it destroyed the deceiver as much as the deceived. "I cannot do this," he said. "Can we not leave it at that for now?"

At his words, she turned a bright pink. "Perhaps I should not have told you that I loved you. I did not mean to tell you. Somehow, the words just slipped out. You were kissing me, and my heart was so full that I—"

She stopped abruptly, and Ben watched her entire posture change. At first weighted down by confusion and hurt, now she donned a sort of armor—one of pride—pride that squared her shoulders and lifted her chin. "I love you," she said, "but that is *my* burden to bear. You need have no fear that because of my sentiments, I will now expect something of you."

"Such a thought never entered my head."

"Of course, it did! You are a wealthy peer. A *premier parti*. This sort of thing must happen to you all the time. Surely this cannot be the first time a female has expressed feelings for you—feelings that are as unwanted as they are unreciprocated."

Ben wanted to curse . . . to swear at the top of his lungs . . . to yell at the situation, and at himself for having been such a fool. "Phoebe, you mistake the matter entirely. Please, allow me to explain."

"Explanations are unnecessary."

"To the contrary, they are quite necessary. Only I am having the devil's own time knowing how to begin."

She waved his words aside. "Tell me nothing, my lord, merely let me have my say. Then allow me to leave with some semblance of dignity."

Short of kissing her, a thing Ben wished he had the courage to do, he knew of no way to stop her from talking.

"I will leave Holden House first thing tomorrow," she said, "and once I am back in Coalport, where I have acquaintances and a job—both of which keep me busy six days out of every week—you may rest assured that I will not be forever showing up on your doorstep. Furthermore, to set your mind at ease, you may come to the village at any time you wish, secure in the knowledge that I will not be lying in wait for you. There will be no 'chance' encounters."

"Phoebe, if you will only listen to—"

"As well," she continued, as if he had not spoken, "you need not fear opening your post, for you will receive no letters from me containing protestations of my undying affection, nor demands for some reciprocal declaration from you."

The firelight was reflected in her eyes, revealing a hint of moisture—a hint that threatened to become a flood at any moment. "And now," she said, "I will bid you a good night."

She took the candle from him, then crossed the room, her head held as high as any queen's. Before she opened the door, however, she paused. She did not turn around, but kept her back to Ben, using her free hand to brush away the tears that had obviously begun to course down her cheeks. "If at some future time you remember this evening, my lord, I beg you will credit my unseemly behavior to the effects of the champagne. As I told you, I have no head for wine."

She said nothing more, merely lifted the latch and opened the door. She had only just crossed the threshold when she stopped suddenly, standing in the doorway as if turned to stone. A moment later, she gasped. "No," she murmured, "it cannot be."

Slowly, she turned and looked back at Ben. He could not read her expression in the dim light, but her posture had gone from regal to rigid, giving him some hint of what lay ahead.

"I must be the greatest fool in nature," she said. "When I was prattling on earlier about our first meeting, and about your deft handling of the champagne glasses, you told me that you had practiced the tactic before your looking glass, in the privacy of your rooms."

Ben offered no response. What could he say?

As if compelled to do so, Phoebe retraced her steps, coming close enough to Ben to search his face. While she looked at him, a noticeable iciness invaded her from head to toe. "You recalled that rather obscure bit of information with such ease, my lord, that I am prompted to inquire if you have been the recipient of some miracle cure."

Not allowing him time to answer, she said, "How happy you must be, for it seems the amnesia resulting from your war injury has healed itself."

At that moment, Ben wished he did, indeed, have amnesia, for how was he to endure the memory of the combined pain and anger in Phoebe's eyes.

"Of course," she continued, "I have never heard of such a thing happening—this sudden remission. Could it be—pray, forgive my suspicious nature—but could your loss of memory have been a complete fabrication?" She looked toward the polar bear rug, the soft fur still showing the indentation where they had lain in one another's arms mere minutes ago. "Could it be that this was all planned?"

Her voice caught on the final word, and unable to deny her accusation, Ben remained silent.

Phoebe swallowed the tears that threatened to choke her. "It was all a sham, was it not? A ruse meant to deceive me into thinking you no longer harbored ill will toward me for refusing you eight years ago?"

"For breaking my heart," he amended quietly.

"Your heart? Have you such an organ? I used to think so. Now, I wonder."

She laughed, but the sound had no humor in it. "What was the plan, my lord? To seduce me, then cast me aside, thereby showing me how it felt to be the one rejected?"

At his silent nod, she closed her eyes, as if the sight of him was too painful to be borne. "So it was true all along. You are a rake."

He flinched as if she had slapped him. "I suppose I deserved that."

"Tell me," she said, "why did you not carry your plan to fruition? Surely no female has ever contributed more willingly to her own destruction than I. What happened? At the last minute, was the thought of making love to me too repugnant, even for a rake?"

"Damnation, Phoebe! Do not even think such a thing. I abandoned the plan because I discovered something I should have known all along. I realized that I wanted something else far more than I wanted revenge. I wanted what we once had. I realized that I still loved you, and I wanted you to love me. When you told me that your heart was, and always had been mine, I—"

"I beg of you, do not mock me by throwing my words in my face! There is not the slightest need, for believe me, I am sufficiently mortified to suit even you."

She turned then and hurried to the door, her sudden movements causing the flame of her candle to sputter, obliging her to shield it with her hand. She stopped once again at the threshold. "Since we have come full circle, my lord, I will give you back the words you spoke to me eight years ago. 'Pray forgive me for having taken up your time. You may rest assured, it will not happen again.'"

Having uttered the words, Phoebe stepped from the room and closed the door softly behind her.

Chapter Fifteen

At the first pink rays of sunrise, Phoebe lit the candle on the washstand. The candle she had used to light her way from the library the evening before had burned itself out long ago, along with the heat of her mortification. Knowing what she must do, she took her cloak from the peg on the wall, threw the dark wool around her shoulders, then fastened the frog at her throat. She had removed the Egyptian costume hours earlier, at which time she had donned her blue merino and her leather boots.

Unfortunately, it had been too dark to leave Holden House at that time, so she had sat on the edge of the narrow cot, praying for first light to come swiftly, and praying as well for the silent tears that ran down her cheeks to end their incessant flow. She knew better than to pray for her broken heart to mend; that pain would need a lifetime to heal.

Now, with the coming of dawn, she draped the green silk costume over her arm, being careful not to drop the gold slippers or the veil. She would return the costume to Miss Constance's room. If the dear lady was awake, Phoebe would tell her good-bye; otherwise, she would write her a note, thanking her for her many kindnesses.

Moving as silently as possible, Phoebe quit the lilac-and-silver bedchamber, tiptoed along the corridor, then made her way down the marble staircase to the vestibule. After climbing the spiral stairs to the landing that gave access to Miss Constance's apartment, Phoebe heard soft snores and knew the elderly lady was asleep.

It was just as well, for Miss Constance would have wanted to know about the dinner with Ben, and Phoebe would have been obliged to pretend that all had gone well. This way, there would be no need for further subterfuge.

After placing the costume on the tooled-leather seaman's chest from which it had come, Phoebe traversed the long room to Miss Constance's dressing table, where she hoped to find a pencil and some writing paper. Like all the other surfaces in the room, the dressing table was piled high with personal items. She pushed aside a silver-backed comb and brush set, a matching pin tray, a long, thin box containing those foot-long hat pins that once secured both hat and wig to a lady's head, and the ceramic pots that held Miss Constance's powder and rouge. Finally, Phoebe found a pencil.

There was no writing paper anywhere in the room, so with only the slightest qualm, Phoebe retrieved a wafered letter that peeked out from under a stack of lace-edged handkerchiefs. The wafer had been broken, so Phoebe merely unfolded the slightly yellowed sheet and wrote her brief note on the blank space beneath the lady's direction.

What made Phoebe turn the paper over, she could not say, but when she did, the first thing she saw was Ben's signature. With the aid of the candlelight, she read the brief lines. It was a letter of condolence from Ben to his great-aunt, a very personal missive, reminding the lady of a time he had visited with her and his great-uncle. The words were written months ago, at the time Ben was supposedly suffering from amnesia, and this reminder of his duplicity started Phoebe's tears anew.

Wanting nothing so much as to be gone from the house, she blew out the candle, propped the letter against the base of the candlestick so Miss Constance would see it first thing, then hurried from the room. Without the light from the candle, the stairwell and the spiral staircase were pitch black, and footing on the wrought-iron treads was uncertain, prompting Phoebe to move carefully, and hold steadfastly to the handrail. She was not overly worried, for she knew she would be safe enough once she reached the vestibule, where she would be able to see.

It never once entered her mind that falling might not be the only danger in the darkness, but when she stepped off the last stair, she realized her error. Noiselessly, a hand reached out and clamped over her mouth. Then a strong arm grabbed her around the waist and pulled her up hard against a broad chest.

A prisoner of her own cloak, her arms were pinned to her sides, and she could not even resist. Thankfully, before she had an opportunity to kick her capturer in the shins, Ben whispered into her ear.

"Forgive me," he said, "but I could not let you go into the vestibule. Abbott and the ghost of my aunt's erstwhile fiancé are in the paneled drawing room, removing paintings from a secret compartment behind the wall, and they must not see you. If they suspect you have discovered their nefarious activities, they might attempt to save their necks by wringing yours."

Phoebe may have been hurt and angry with Ben, but in that moment she was more than happy to know it was his arm around her waist, and not the arm of the lout who had manhandled her in the kitchen. Ben might be a rake, but he was not a cutthroat, and when she pushed lightly against the hand that covered her mouth, he released her.

"Thank you," she said stiffly. "It is fortunate for me that you happened to be down here, otherwise I might have walked right into their midst."

"Nothing fortunate about it," Ben said. "I am here by design."

Phoebe turned quickly, but it was still too dark to see more than the outline of Ben's face. "This is what you meant earlier when you said that Abbott had plans for this evening."

"It is. For that reason, after you left the library I made a great show of returning to my bedchamber. I moved about the room, dropping shoes and slamming doors, to make it appear I was getting ready to retire. Then, after an hour of total quiet, I made my way to one of the bedchambers that overlooks the stable yard. I sat beside that darkened window for perhaps another hour before the stable door finally opened and a smallish man I have never seen before drove a carter's wagon out into the stable yard.

"That wagon, and a deep-sided farm wagon, are waiting there now, piled high with items. And even though they are covered over by thick canvases, which reveal nothing, I have no doubt the wagons are filled with furnishings taken from this house. As we speak, Abbott and the man whom I assume you met in the kitchen are loading the artwork onto another farm wagon. That is why, when I heard you leave your bedchamber, I followed you. I could not let you walk into harm's way."

Just knowing that Ben cared enough not to let harm come to her caused the tears to spring to her eyes, but she quickly brushed them aside. For her heart's sake, she would be wise not to dwell on this one kindness. Far better to concentrate on the thievery afoot, and the loss of the family treasures hidden beneath those canvas-covered wagons.

"Ben. You cannot let them steal the Holden House furnishings."

"I have no intention of doing so."

Hearing the determination behind his words, Phoebe caught her bottom lip between her teeth. She had said that he must not let those men steal his family legacy, but until his reply, she had not considered the risks involved in reclaiming those furnishings. Ben could be injured, or worse. He was only one man, while there were three thieves on the premises. "Do you have your pocket pistol?"

"I do. Unfortunately, it will do me no good at the moment."

"Why not?"

"Firstly, it is not as easy as you might think to take another human life. And secondly, the pistol fires only two shots, and there are three men. If I should employ both shots to their optimum capacity, that would still leave one man, who might well possess a pistol of his own."

Ben could not see Phoebe's face, but when she grabbed hold of his lapels, he knew she was concerned for his safety. "Never fear. I have no intention of letting any of that trio use me for target practice." He covered her hands with his. "Especially not now."

When Phoebe stiffened, then eased her hands from his, Ben knew better than to press the matter. Instead, he told her his plan. "Yesterday, when I discovered that the snow had melted sufficiently to make the roads travelable, it occurred to me that if the three miscreants had the least intelligence, they would make their move sometime before dawn."

"And that is why you sent a message to your uncle's solicitor to bring the constable from Coalport as soon a possible?"

"It is. Every minute the trio remain here, they are in danger of discovery, and they know it. Therefore, it be-

ooves them to unearth their cache of ill-gotten gains
nd leave Holden House at the first opportunity."

"What of the constable? Perhaps you should wait
ntil he arrives."

"I should like nothing better. Unfortunately, there is
o time to wait. I am persuaded the thieves will at-
empt to drive the wagons to Shrewsbury, for it is a
narket town, where strangers are not so noticeable. If
hey should reach the town, both men and wagons
vill be harder to trace. Besides," he added, "my valet
s waiting on the Shrewsbury road, armed and ready."

"Your valet?"

"Fortson. He arrived yesterday, and together we de-
ermined that it would be a tactical error to try to de-
ain the thieves while still at the house, where there
ire any number of hiding places, not to mention inno-
ent people who might be hurt. Much better to let
hem leave, then stop them on the road."

"But a valet. Surely the constable would be a more
eliable assistant."

"Actually, Fortson is a most capable fellow. He and
 were in the Peninsula together. I trust him with my
ife, and I know from experience that he and I will be
nore than a match for three unsuspecting malefac-
ors."

"You know from exper— Oh, yes. I almost forgot,
ou never really had amnesia, did you?"

A muted thump sounded quite near the concealed
loor in the vestibule wall, saving Ben from embracing
he topic of his supposed memory loss, a topic that
eeded more time, and a lot more space than was avail-
ible at the moment. "Shh," he said, pulling Phoebe with
im into the pitch-darkness under the spiral stairs.
'Someone is coming."

The words had only just left his mouth when the
spring clicked and the door popped open. "Here," the
all, slender man on the other side of the door said,

holding out a medium-size painting to someone in the vestibule. "This is the last one. As soon as it is put on the wagon and secured, you and your wife can leave. Bill, too, if his wagon is ready."

"Right. And what'll you be doing?" Henry Abbott asked. "Whilst Bill and me's doing all the work?"

"Lower your voice, you gin-soaked cretin, and just do as you're told. There's one more thing I mean to take with me. It's mine, and I'll not leave without it."

"Sommit else?" Abbott said. "What with the three wagon loads last month, and these three today, b'ain nothing left. We got it all. The furniture, the paintings even the silver. What's left, save the sheets 'is lordship be sleeping on? You must 'ate 'im real bad to want to steal everything."

"It's his uncle I hate," the man said. "The previous Lord Holden. As for stealing from this one, how can i be stealing, when by rights everything here should have been mine?"

By rights? The man must be deranged. Ben knew for a fact that aside from himself and Aunt Constance there were no more Holdens. And certainly no more heirs.

Having gained one more insight into the mind of the man he was dealing with, Ben slipped his hand around to the pistol, ready to draw the weapon if need be. He hoped it would not become necessary, not with Phoebe standing just behind him. And yet, with a crazy man moving about freely, especially one who had proven himself a bully twice over, Ben felt he must be prepared for any eventuality.

"Do as I tell you!" the man ordered Abbott. "Then be on your way. I'll catch up with you as soon as I've gotten back my family's property."

At the man's raised voice, Abbott had taken a discreet step back, but now he reached out for the painting. "I'll do it," he grumbled, "but soon as I gets my share of the money, b'aint nobody giving me orders again. Nobody."

While Abbott went toward the kitchen area, the other man entered the stairwell, leaving the door ajar. The pale light coming from the vestibule was sufficient to light his way up the spiral staircase, but not bright enough to reveal the two dark-clad figures hidden beneath the stairs.

Phoebe had remained perfectly still behind Ben, but now he felt her touch his hand. Her fingers were like icicles. "Ben," she whispered very close to his ear, "Miss Constance is up there."

"I know," he whispered back.

Since the man was obviously familiar with the passages in this rabbit-warren of a house, both the secret and the not-so-secret ones, Ben had hoped the fellow meant to go only to the landing at the top of the spiral stairs, then exit into the corridor. Unfortunately, that was not to be. The man had no sooner reached the platform than he pushed open the door to Constance Holden's apartment.

Scarce two seconds later, Ben heard his great-aunt's voice. She sounded more outraged than frightened. "Jamie Whitcombe," she said, "how dare you enter my bedchamber uninvited? Go away, for I do not allow gentlemen callers abovestairs. Not even gentlemen ghosts."

"I'll go," the man said, "for I've no wish to be here. First, though, I'll have the Whitcombe betrothal ring. By rights it's mine."

"You want your ring back? But, why, Jamie? Through all the years you were away, I remained true to my promise to you."

The man made a scoffing sound. "A lot your promise was worth, you crazy old hag. My grandfather had not even left the country before your brother wrote to tell him the engagement was off."

"Your grandfather? What on earth do you mean?"

"His lordship said you were underage," the man continued, ignoring Constance Holden's question. "He said he would never consent to such a misalliance. Claimed a Whitcombe was not a suitable match for a Holden."

"No!" Constance said, her voice filled with outrage. "It cannot be. Roland would not do such a thing to me, to his only sister. He knew how much I loved you—loved Jamie."

"Not suitable," the fellow repeated, "as if everyone in the county didn't know the Holdens all had bats in their belfries."

Ben flinched at the familiar taunt, and though he waited for a similar response from Phoebe, it did not come.

"Crazy as a loon, his high-and-mighty lordship was, yet he kept the betrothal ring right enough. Refused to return it. Even when my grandfather came home from the colonies, and made a special trip to Holden House to get the ring, so's he could give it to his new bride, my grandmother, his lordship sent him away. Threatened to call the constable if Grandfather ever set foot on the property again."

Ben heard a strangled sound come from his great-aunt. "Jamie was here? And Roland sent him away?"

"That ruby was all my family had, and without it, we've been obliged to do all manner of things just to survive."

"My Jamie was here? Alive and well? And married to another?"

Whitcombe cursed, and from the anger in the man's voice, Ben knew he could wait no longer. He must go up to his aunt's apartment. Who could tell what such a man had in mind. If Aunt Constance screamed, he might try to silence her, and all for that insignificant little ruby.

"Stay here," he whispered into Phoebe's ear. "No matter what you hear, remain hidden."

At Phoebe's nod, Ben squeezed her hand. Then he crept up the spiral stairs, his pistol pointed and ready.

The moment he stepped onto the landing, and looked inside the apartment, he saw his aunt sitting in a slipper chair pulled up to the window. Jamie Whitcombe's grandson stood in front of her, and though Ben could not see what the fellow was doing, it looked as though he were holding Aunt Constance's hand.

"Ouch!" Aunt Constance said. "That hurts. Unhand me, you . . . you villain."

"Satan take me!" the man said, trying to force open the elderly lady's clinched fist. "You're as crazy as your brother. Give me the demmed ring, or I'll take it, finger and all."

"Unhand the lady," Ben said, "or Satan will be coming for you even sooner than anticipated."

Like a man deranged, Whitcombe continued to pry Constance Holden's fingers open, even though Ben had pointed the plistol at him and pulled the hammer back. "You have three seconds to move aside, knave. Fail to heed my warning, and you are a dead man!"

From her hiding place beneath the spiral staircase, Phoebe heard the exchange. Unfortunately, she could not tell exactly what was happening. All she knew with any certainty was that Miss Constance had cried out, and that Ben had given the thief three seconds to comply or die. She had never been so frightened in her life—not for herself, but for Ben. What if he shot the man, then had to stand trial for murder?

Or worse yet, what if the man shot Ben?

"One," Ben said. "Two. Th—"

"Hey! What's this?" the man said suddenly, his voice more like that of a petulant child than of a grown man's. "You Holdens are trying to mugger me out of what's mine. Trying to cheat me again. Where's the real ring, old woman? This paltry thing isn't the Whitcombe ruby."

"I know nothing of the Whitcombe ruby," Miss Constance said, her tone frigid enough to snub a duke, "but that is the ring put on my finger by Jamie Whitcombe. I was blinded by love, so I never questioned the size of the gem. Now, of course, I wish I had never seen it or him! And believe me, sirrah, should I live to be a *very* old woman, I hope never again to set eyes on you."

Hurrah for Miss Constance!

"But, but," the man sputtered, "this stone can't be worth more than fifty quid. My grandfather—"

"Lied," Ben said. "Like the proverbial fish that got away, it would appear the size of the stone grew with the telling."

"Don't you say that!" the man yelled. "My grandfa wouldn't lie to me!"

Suddenly there was the sound of running feet, then a shot rang out, and something heavy hit the floor.

Phoebe's heart leapt into her throat. She told herself not to jump to conclusions, but a gun had gone off, someone had fallen, and the man who had just stepped out onto the landing was not Ben!

Jamie Whitcombe's grandson stood at the top of the stairs. His face had a wild look, and his mouth was pulled into a snarl like that of a cornered badger. He held something in the palm of his hand, and after staring at it for a moment, he uttered a vile oath, then threw whatever it was against the wall.

There was a soft, metallic *plink*. Then the object fell to the floor below, the insignificant sound of its landing out of all proportion to the rage of the man who had thrown it. After another oath, Whitcombe bounded down the wrought-iron steps.

Where was Ben? What had happened to him? Was he in-

jured? Was he dead? No! Please, God, do not let him be dead!

Phoebe wanted to scream Ben's name. Unfortunately, fear and rage had combined to render her lungs useless, and though she tried to draw air into those organs, nothing happened. She had lost the ability to breathe, but if it was the last thing she did in this lifetime, she would stop the villain on the stairs.

He had reached the fourth from the bottom stair when Phoebe reached through the back of the wrought-iron riser and grabbed his ankles, holding on with all her might. Her determination, plus the momentum of Whitcombe's flight, sent the man flying headfirst. The top of his head hit the wall with a most unpleasant thud; after which, he crumpled to the floor like a rag-stuffed doll.

"Phoebe!" Ben yelled from the landing.

"I am here!"

Ben took the stairs two at a time. Whitcombe lay unmoving, sprawled across the final two steps, so Ben merely grabbed the stair rail with both hands and leapt over it. He landed just in front of Phoebe, who threw herself into his arms.

"My love," he said, "are you injured?"

She shook her head. Still struggling for breath, she said, "The gun . . . I heard . . . then Whitcombe . . ." Too shaken even to give voice to what she had feared was true, she burst into tears.

Ben held her close for a full minute, allowing her her well-earned release, then he gave her a shortened version of what had occurred in his aunt's apartment. "The fool ran at me," he said, "and the pistol discharged. Aunt Constance fell to the ground, and before I could give chase, I had to ascertain whether or not she had been struck by the bullet."

Phoebe pushed away so she could look up at him. "Is she—"

"Merely fainted," he replied.

Phoebe would have liked to return to Ben's arms, but he placed his hands on her shoulders and stepped away from her. "We must talk, my love, but now is not the appropriate time. I cannot be sure if the other two villains heard the pistol shot. If they did, they may even now be inside the house, looking for this fellow."

Phoebe stared at Whitcombe, who still had not moved. She, who had never so much as raised her hand to another human being, had managed to hurt this fellow twice. Horrified at what might be the repercussions of her act, she said, "Did I do murder?"

Ben bent and felt the man's neck. "He lives yet," he said, a touch of humor finding its way into his voice. "But if he has any brains left in his head, he will not tangle with you a third time."

Phoebe was in no frame of mind to be teased, but she let it pass for the moment, much too relieved to know that the man was only unconscious.

Ben's manner grew serious again. "If I leave you here with Whitcombe, while I go in search of the other two, do you think you could find something with which to tie his hands and feet?"

At her nod, Ben grabbed Whitcombe's legs and dragged them off the steps so Phoebe could go up to his aunt's apartment to search out a rope. "Be careful," he said softly.

She paused halfway to the landing, turning back for one last look at Ben. "And you," she added, the words so soft they might have been a prayer.

After Ben slipped out the secret door and closed it behind him, Phoebe hurried up to the apartment. Ben had carried his aunt over to her bed, and at Phoebe's entrance the elderly lady sat up. "My dear," she said. "Jamie's grandson. Where is he?"

"I am afraid, ma'am, that he is lying at the bottom

of the spiral staircase. He . . . he tripped and fell, and now he is unconscious."

"Good. He is not a nice man."

Suddenly realizing that with this man's revelations, all Miss Constance's dreams for the future would die, Phoebe went to her friend and took her hands. "I am so sorry, ma'am, that your Jamie wed another."

"As to that, my dear, I realize now that Jamie and I would not have suited. A person wants real stamina to be a Holden, and Jamie gave up far too easily. And . . . and I am happy the engagement is finally at an end. Now I am free to entertain other offers."

Trying not to smile, Phoebe hugged the lady's thin shoulders. "Ma'am, you are a constant source of joy."

"I am?"

"Most definitely. Now, however, I must see to Whitcombe. I need to bind his hands and feet before he comes to himself."

She walked over to the leather seaman's chest, where she had left the Egyptian costume, and retrieved the gold rope she had worn around her waist. "This should do," she said. "Now if only I could find something to use for a weapon."

"A weapon? My dear, whatever for?"

"Once I make certain Whitcombe is unable to follow us, I intend to find your nephew. Abbott and another man are still out there, and Ben has only one bullet left in his pistol."

Apparently needing no time to think, Miss Constance hurried over to her dressing table, where she lifted a long, thin box from among the clutter. She brought the box to Phoebe. "I should think one of these would do."

The box contained several jewel-knobbed hat pins, some more than a foot long. "If the wind is strong," Miss Constance said, "and a lady's chapeau does not tie beneath her chin, she needs a pin long enough to go through both her hat and her wig, to secure every-thing to her own hair." She laughed lightly. "When I was a girl, one of my beaux referred to such pins as miniature swords."

The contents of the box certainly looked wicked enough to be used as weapons, and because Phoebe had no notion where she might find anything even half so lethal looking, she chose the longest hat pin in the box. At either end of the pin were garnet knobs. The knob at the top of the pin was stationary, while the matching knob at the pointed end slipped on and off—its purpose to protect any person so foolish as to get too close to a lady's chapeau. Making certain both the pretty garnets were in place, Phoebe slipped the hat pin up inside the long sleeve of her dress.

After returning to Whitcombe, and binding his hands behind his back, she looped the rope through the bottom stair for good measure. Then she tied his feet as well. Confident that the prisoner could not escape, even if he should regain consciousness, Phoebe opened the secret door and slipped quietly out into the vestibule.

Chapter Sixteen

Phoebe moved soundlessly down the back corridor to the kitchen. Finding that room empty, she tiptoed across the stone floor to peek out the rear window.

Two canvas-covered farm wagons stood waiting in the stable yard. To each wagon was hitched a pair of draft horses. The poor animals, obviously tired of standing about in the cold morning air, alternated between tossing their massive heads impatiently and pawing the ground in search of any grass hidden beneath the snow. Of the carter's wagon, there was no sign, and Phoebe breathed a sign of relief, happy to know that only one villain remained on the premises.

The rising sun had turned the dawn sky from a striped pink to a clear, light blue, and dozens of boot prints were visible leading to the stable doors. Ben was nowhere in sight, nor were Henry and Mary Abbott, and because the stable doors were closed, some sixth sense told Phoebe that she would find everyone there.

Using the wagons as cover, she moved as quietly as possible across the snow, not stopping until she was mere inches from the stables. The doors were slightly ajar, and by standing in just the right spot, she could peer through the resulting crack. Mary and Henry Abbott were completely visible, their backs to the door. Ben was there as well, some twenty feet away. He faced the couple, his pistol pointed toward Abbott's head. Unfortunately, the butler held an ancient blunderbuss in his right hand, the short barrel pointed directly at Ben's chest.

The confrontation might have been a stalemate, had Abbott not increased his advantage by coiling his large beefy arm around Trudy's throat, holding the young maid in front of him like a shield.

"Let the girl go," Ben said, his tone brooking no refusal.

"Not bloody likely," Abbott replied. "Not 'til you toss your barker into yonder stall."

Even at a distance, Phoebe's nose told her that the servant had boosted his courage by imbibing liberally in blue ruin.

When Ben did not comply with Abbott's suggestion to toss his pistol aside, the lout tightened his hold on the young maid's throat, causing her to gasp for breath.

"Henry!" Mary Abbott said. "You're choking the child. Let her go."

"Can't do it, Mags. It's me or 'is lordship, and the minute I let Trudy 'ere go, 'e'll let me 'ave it between me eyes."

"Henry, please!"

"Sorry, pet, but I b'aint ready to die. Not just yet. Not now there's big money coming to me."

"I'm your wife," Mary said, "and I've stuck by you for eleven years. But I'll have no part in murder, and I'll not stand by and see that child killed. Either you let her go, or I stay here."

"Stay 'ere? 'Ave you turned Bedlamite on me, Mags? You stay 'ere, and you'll be transported. Or worse."

"Even so, I'll not spend eternity with that child's life on my conscious."

"Let Trudy go," Ben said again. "Release her, then drop your weapon to the floor. You and I both know the reason you have not fired it so far is that your chances of hitting me at this distance are almost nonexistent."

"Please," Mary begged. "Do as his lordship says."

"Listen to your wife, Abbott. Do not be a fool. Whitcombe has met with an accident, and will not be joining you, and the other fellow has fled, probably right into the arms of my man, who is fully armed and waiting on the Shrewsbury road."

"It's a lie."

Ben shook his head. "You are alone, Abbott."

The large man, resembling nothing so much as a cornered hare, glanced toward his wife, who covered her face with her hands, then turned her back on her husband.

Ben took one step forward, prompting Abbott to take one step back, toward the doors.

"Use what is left of that pickled brain of yours," Ben said. "Release the girl, then just turn around and walk out of here. You have my word on it, no one will attempt to stop you. However, if Trudy is injured, I promise you, I will see you hanged."

Phoebe watched Abbott take another step back, then another, until he was very close to the double doors. He still held Trudy in front of him, and the blunderbuss was still pointed at Ben.

Not nearly as confident as her beloved that Abbott's shot would not find its aim, Phoebe drew the hat pin out of her dress sleeve, ready to use whatever means necessary to ensure Ben's and Trudy's safety. After tossing away the movable knob, she stepped to the left of the door, out of sight, then waited.

"Last chance, Mags," Abbott said, pushing the door open with his backside, "come with me, luv."

While he looked at his wife, waiting for her answer, he took one more step back, and Phoebe seized what she was certain was her one opportunity. She tight-

ened her fingers around the hat pin, drew back her
arm, then drove the slender steel shank directly into
Abbott's left buttock.

The man yelled like a stuck pig. For an instant, he
did not move; then, dropping the blunderbuss, he released the terrified maid, who ran back into the stables. Using both his freed hands, Abbott grasped his
wounded *derriere* and fell to the ground, shrieking in
pain.

Ben heard the scream, and was at the door almost
as soon as the big man hit the ground, his pistol
raised and ready to fire if necessary. What he saw
stopped him in his tracks, for there was Abbott
writhing on the ground, while Phoebe stood over
him, a horrified expression in her lovely eyes, and a
long hat pin in her hand, the sharp tip suspiciously
red.

Very gently, Ben caught her wrist and removed the
bloodied weapon from her unresisting hand. Then,
while keeping his pistol aimed at Abbott, Ben took
Phoebe into his arms. She clung to him for some time,
her face buried against his chest. When she finally
ceased to tremble, Ben kissed her forehead, then
asked her if she would be so good as to take the
frightened maid back into the house.

"But what of you? What if the other one comes
back?"

"Darling girl," Ben said, "in view of the fates that
have befallen his partners in crime, the fellow would
be a fool to come within ten miles of you."

It was late afternoon before Phoebe joined Miss
Constance in her apartment. Trudy had finally re-
gained her composure and had done her best to pre-
pare a tea tray, which she had brought up to the two
grateful ladies. By that time, the three females were
the only people left in the house, for everyone else

was in Coalport, either at the gaol or at Mrs. Curdy's, where Ben had promised to deliver Mary Abbott until time for the trial.

What seemed an eternity earlier, the constable and Mr. McNeese, Roland Holden's solicitor, had arrived on horseback. Ben had met them in the stable yard, where they remained, listening to his version of the events of the morning. Before long, the valet, the inimitable Fortson, drove up. The feisty little Scotsman had Whitcombe's accomplice wrapped up in a canvas and tied to the back of the carter's wagon.

It being cold out, they had all retired to the relative warmth of the kitchen, and for a time it seemed that pandemonium reigned belowstairs, with the constable asking questions of first one person, then the other, and two of the thwarted miscreants begging for medical attention. Finally, when all the preliminary questions were asked and answered, the farm wagons were returned to the stables, and the carter's wagon was unloaded so it would accommodate Whitcombe, Abbott, and the man called Bill on their trip to the village.

Ben had put the dappled gray to the sleigh, and with Mary Abbott sitting beside him, he followed the wagon and the two horsemen past the low stone wall and down the lane, toward the iron bridge that crossed the blue waters of the Severn.

Just before he left, however, Ben caught Phoebe's hand and pulled her close so he might whisper something in her ear. "Stay here," he said, "until I return."

Though it was exactly what Phoebe wanted to do, she took umbrage at his tone. "And why should I remain here, my lord?"

"Because," he replied, giving her a searching look that left her as giddy as a schoolroom chit, "you and I have unfinished business, and eight years is quite long enough to leave it so."

Holden House, eight weeks later . . .

Ben found Phoebe sitting at the handsome rosewood desk in the master bedchamber. The candles
were lit in the pretty cobalt blue candelabra, and by
their light his bride read a three-week-old newspaper.
"Listen to this account of the trial," she said. "'Lord
Holden's fiancée, Miss Phoebe Lowell, was a guest at
Holden House during the attempted theft. Unfortunately, she spent her entire time in company with his
lordship's great-aunt, and saw nothing of the malefactors; therefore, she was not called to testify before the
court.'"

Disgusted, Phoebe threw the newspaper onto the
desk. "Reading this, a person would be forgiven for
thinking I hid beneath the bed, trembling in fear."

"You? Afraid? Ha!" Ben closed the bedchamber
door, then crossed the room to stand beside the large
tester bed, with its fresh, new rose satin hangings.
"Had you been with Wellington in the Peninsula, my
love, I am persuaded Napoleon would have surren-
dered at least a year earlier."

Though Phoebe knew her husband was merely
teasing her, she smiled, pleased to know that he did
not think her a coward. She was pleased as well to be
wearing another of Miss Constance's wedding gifts, a
beautifully sewn, ivory-colored night rail trimmed in
blond lace. Knowing the delight her husband took in
seeing her in each new ensemble, she straightened the
ribbons that held the confection in place.

She could hear Ben just behind her. He was busy removing his coat, his waistcoat, and his top boots. Still
wearing his breeches, his shirt, and his cravat, he
moved to the desk, leaned down, then placed a warm
kiss at the nape of her neck. "I missed you," he said.
"This getting to know the tenants is eating into my
time with my beautiful bride."

His lips moved from her nape to a sensitive spot he had discovered just behind her left ear, sending shivers of delight down her spine.

"I am very proud of you," she said, her voice not quite steady. "You are proving to be a very good landowner."

His strong hands moved slowly down her arms, then back up again, igniting little brushfires of desire that flared throught her body. "What do you say we adjourn to that lovely big bed, my sweet, where I can show you just how good I can be?"

"As you tried that first night, when I took refuge from the snowstorm?"

He put his hand beneath her elbow and bid her stand, then he rested his hands on her hips and drew her close against him, fitting her back snugly against his chest. "What a night that was."

"Umm," she murmured. "You crawled into my bed and pulled me close against you, much as you are doing now. And when I felt the warmth of your naked body, I thought you were a dream."

He chuckled. "And I thought you were a serving wench from the tavern, come to warm my bed."

"How disappointed you must have been when you discovered it was me."

"Disappointed? Never. From the first moment I realized it was truly you, and that you were not some figment of my overheated imagination, I knew that my heart was in peril. Then, before I quite knew how it had come about, I wanted nothing so much as to surrender not only my heart, but also my soul. I positively ached to give them into your keeping."

He drew her hips closer still, so that she was aware of his need for her. "Much as I ache now."

"Sir," she said, feigning shock, "how like you to take liberties when I am unable to evade them."

"Very like me," he said, his warm breath teasing a

loose curl at her ear, "for my timing was always im-
peccable."

"Practiced, I have no doubt, on thousands of willing females."

He faked a discreet cough. "As to that, my love, a
gentleman never tells."

"Gentleman! Sir, you are every inch the rake!"

"And you love it!"

"I do not."

"No? Shall I prove it to you?"

"No," she said, moving out of his reach. "You mean
to kiss me, because you know that I cannot resist you.
Which only proves what a rake you are."

"Very true," he said, sighing as if he regretted his
rakishness. "I am a total blackguard. A soulless wretch.
Do you suppose there is any hope that I might be re-
deemed?"

While he asked the question, he moved to where
she stood and began slowly untying the ribbon that
held the lace night rail in place. After slipping the
confection from her shoulders, he lowered his head
and began placing slow kisses along the side of her
neck, then across her collarbone, and down to the soft,
tempting swell of her breasts.

He let his lips linger for a time in the tantalizing
valley between her breasts, then he lifted his head. "I
want to kiss your lips," he whispered. "Then, when I
have had my fill, I want you to remove my cravat and
my shirt, and kiss me as I just kissed you."

Phoebe, finding nothing to dislike in that totally
rakish suggestion, unfastened the cravat at her
beloved's neck. "First," she said, kissing the strong
column of his throat, "you must tell me how much
you love me."

He muttered a mild oath, as if much put upon,
though his bride was not deceived. "What a perfect
pair we are," he said. "You a creature who needs reas-

urance, and me a creature who refuses to explain his
ctions."

With that, he lifted her in his arms, carried her to
he bed, then laid her down very gently.

"Trust me," she said, reaching up to pull him down
eside her, "after almost three weeks of marriage, this
articular action needs no explanation."

Ben laughed aloud, then he leaned down and
laimed her lips in a kiss that sent Phoebe's heart
oaring. "My beautiful angel," he said, "I love you
nore than I can ever say. And every day I thank
Heaven for sending you back into my life."

"And I thank Heaven," she said, "for giving me
ack my beloved rake."

Phoebe worked the ends of Ben's shirt free of his
reeches, then lifted the linen over his head. As happened every time, her breath caught in her throat at
ight of his broad shoulders and the beautiful muscles
n his arms. Just as he had requested, she rained
isses over his warm chest; then, impatient to have
im kiss her again, she licked her lips in that way he
laimed drove him wild.

When he moaned, she smiled, enjoying the knowl-
dge that she excited him every bit as much as he exited her. "And now, my handsome rake, if you
would not have me perish from longing, I beg of you,
iss me again."

Always happy to oblige, her husband gathered her
n his arms and gave her what they both wanted.

Author's Note

Ironbridge, the first iron bridge in the world, wa built in 1779, across the Severn River, near Coalbrook dale. The area is regarded by many historians as the birthplace of the Industrial Revolution. In the Severn valley, around Coalbrookdale, in a quiet corner of Shropshire, were woods ideal for making charcoal, as well as deposits of iron, clay, and accessible coal seams—all the necessary ingredients for developing industry.

In 1707, in this mostly rural landscape, Abraham Darby, iron master of a small blast furnace in Coal brookdale, began experimenting with using coke to smelt the local iron. Darby's success ultimately revo lutionized the manufacture of iron and steel. In 1775 Abraham Darby II built the Horsehay Iron Works and later a pottery works. In 1779, Abraham Darby II built the Iron Bridge. An engineering masterpiece of its day, the bridge still stands, though it is no longer used for anything but foot traffic.

The pottery factory no longer exists, but much of the pottery and porcelain produced there has sur vived, and these pieces are prized by today's collector

About the Author

Martha Kirkland has been active in the music and drama scene for most of her life. Serious about her lessons and performances, several years ago she was bitten by the *whimsy* bug and decided to give tap dancing a try. It was love at first shuffle, shuffle, hop, which proves that adage about it never being too late to do what you really want to do. A lifelong resident of Atlanta, her family includes one husband and two daughters.

Martha enjoys hearing from her fans. Letters may be sent to NAL/Signet, or through her Web site:

www.rakehell.com/marthakirkland/home.html